THE MIDNIGHT BOY

A Percy St.-John Mystery

THE
MIDNIGHT
BOY

A Verity Long Mystery

E.A. Allen

THE MIDNIGHT BOY

A Percy St.-John Mystery

HistriaYA

Las Vegas ◊ London ◊ New York ◊ Palm Beach

Published in the United States of America by
Histria Books
7181 N. Hualapai Way, Ste. 130-86
Las Vegas, NV 89166 USA
HistriaBooks.com

HistriaYA is an imprint of Histria Books dedicated to incredible books for Young Adult readers. Titles published under the imprints of Histria Books are distributed in the United States and Canada by Simon & Schuster and worldwide through Unified Book Distribution. We appreciate your support of copyright by purchasing an authorized edition of this book and for respecting intellectual property laws by not reproducing, scanning, or otherwise distributing any part of it by any means without permission. You are supporting authors and enabling Histria Books to continue publishing books for everyone.

All rights reserved. No part of this book may be reprinted or reproduced or utilized in any form or by any electronic, mechanical or other means, now known or hereafter invented, including photocopying and recording, or in any information storage or retrieval system, without the permission in writing from the Publisher. No part of this book may be used or reproduced in any manner for the purpose of training artificial intelligence technologies or systems.

First Edition

Library of Congress Control Number: 2024953104

ISBN 978-1-59211-590-7 (softbound)
ISBN 978-1-59211-612-6 (eBook)

Copyright © 2026 by E.A. Allen

"Hell is empty and all the devils are here."

— William Shakespeare, *The Tempest*

PART ONE
FAREWELL REVEREND LOVECROFT

CHAPTER ONE
WHEREIN I AM AN ORPHAN

Brixley, Surrey. November 1906

1

You'll probably want to know how my father's murder changed my life and made me an expert cracksman. I don't much like to talk about it, but then it's an important story. It's also a pretty complicated story, and as I look back on things — how I survived some hard times and then found my life's work — I am struck by the odd twists and turns that finally led me to Special Branch and then on to Paris and the Deuxième Bureau. But I'm getting ahead of myself. Better to start at the sad events that forced me into life on my own.

My father — Reverend Clarence St.-John — was vicar of the small parish of Brixley, in Surrey. He was murdered one evening as he returned from visiting a sick widow in the neighborhood. I think it was thieves who killed him because his silver cross went missing. Still, no one was ever caught as far as I know and so the villains are enjoying whatever they got for the cross. I haven't forgotten, however, and I have made it one of my life's goals to find them and then... well, I'll know what to do when I've found them.

After my father's funeral, my grandfather made it clear he'd have nothing to do with me. I'll have more to say about him later also, but for now, you need to know that he hated my father because he married my mother — a woman my grandfather considered beneath his son. My grandfather punished us all by having nothing to do with my father — his own son. He hated me too, I guess because I was my mother's son.

My father and I were all alone. My mother had died giving birth to me and so I never knew her. Father told me she was a fine woman who looked forward to loving me very much. And it was she who gave me my name. Percival — you know, after the knight who searched for the Holy Grail. Still, everyone always just called me Percy.

When my grandfather rejected me, the leaders of Brixley didn't know what to do with me, but they soon decided to send me off to a London orphanage. It's called Saint Cuthbert's Asylum for Orphaned and Delinquent Boys, but mainly it's a prison for boys. I don't think the Brixley folks knew that because the man who directed Saint Cuthbert's — the Reverend Mortimer Lovecroft — made such a great show of being saintly and kind to boys.

Police Constable Meeks of Brixley and Mr. Stanton, the President of the Parish Council, forced me into a coach. Meeks tied my hands — because I had already tried to run away — and we were off to London without so much as a goodbye. I think they were ashamed of the way they dealt with me. The journey took all night and so we arrived at the great oaken gates of St. Cuthbert's just at dawn. A thick fog hung low over the big gray block of the building and made it look even more sinister than it truly is. We waited for the longest time, before the gate opened to admit our coach into the prison's outer court. I call it a "prison" from habit. That's what all the boys called it because we did not like to give it the credit of being anything but a place where the London County Council locked up unwanted boys.

As soon as our coach stopped, one of the warders opened the door and helped Meeks drag me out and into the cold, damp air. Mr. Stanton and Meeks followed the warder as he pulled me by my rope, down a narrow passage, and then to a door, which opened to the study of the Reverend Lovecroft — Superintendent of St. Cuthbert's.

2

St. Cuthbert's lies in the environs of London and is a public institution, supported by tax payments from the London County Council. Of course, they accept private charity as well, but mainly the local ratepayers pay it for. I don't mind telling you that supporting orphans is not a priority with the local politicians, and so mainly the orphanage operated on very little money, public or private.

All this history is necessary for my story; else I would not trouble you with the sad state of funding for orphans. I'm not looking for any sympathy. It's just that no money meant no food, or not much anyway. And what food there was, was Gawdawful. But that's a story for later too.

3

As the door opened to Reverend Mortimer Lovecroft's study, I could see only a dark figure sitting in shadows behind a large desk. When he leaned into the light given by a small lamp on the desk, we saw a man dressed all in black, with a thin face with side-whiskers, a hairless head, a long beaky nose, large ears, and birdlike eyes that seemed to seize me in an icy grip.

"This lad is Percy St.-John, sir," said Meeks. "From Brixley, eh?"

"Oh yes. Master St.-John. Oh yes," said Lovecroft standing slowly. He was even taller than I had at first thought. "We've been expecting you. Hold out our hands, if you please, Master St.-John."

I did so, with my palms down, and suddenly there appeared in Lovecroft's hand a rod. He brought it down on my hands and I let out a scream like a lost soul. Meeks jumped back, I guess thinking that Lovecroft would come after him next.

I was in too much pain to ask what the rod was all about. But Reverend Lovecroft explained anyway.

"That Master St.-John is just a foretaste of the pain you'll feel if you step out of line just once while you reside here at St. Cuthbert's. Just once; do you understand me?" he growled through clenched teeth. "Just once."

CHAPTER TWO
WHEREIN EVIL MAKES ITS CHOICE

London
Three Months Earlier

1

The tall shadow moved slowly down the alley, accompanied only by a flurry of old newspapers blown about by the wind. He paused briefly at a door, much like the other doors at the backs of drab buildings, then not bothering to open it, moved swiftly through it as if it were not even there.

Inside, there was neither room nor corridor, as one might have expected, but rather an endless dark fog and a vast realm marked only by the distant screams of the suffering. The shadow paused, as if waiting for instructions before proceeding. Soon a powerful voice spoke through the mist.

"So, you have come, Ozmondura."

"Yes, my lord? As I was told."

"He is coming."

"Oh? Who is that, my lord?"

"Fate will move him into your sphere of action. You must be on your alert, because he is powerful. So powerful and so inspired that he may even be able to defeat you. You must be prepared for him!"

"Do I have the power to destroy him, my lord?"

"No, unfortunately. He is not one of ours. He is one of the others. But you may trick him and divert him and that is what you must do."

"Divert?"

"His fate is moving him directly in the path of my interests. He is even now proceeding in a direction that will block me. DO YOU HEAR ME! ON HIS PRESENT COURSE HE WILL DISRUPT MY INTERESTS!"

2

The shadow cringed and fell back — a painful spasm at the deafening sound of the voice.

"But, my lord, who is this creature? How will I know him?"

"Never mind that, fool, you will know him when he emerges. He will frighten you with his power. But you must nerve yourself."

"You say that he opposes our interests?"

"Ha! He does not even know that he does, but he will come to act in such a way as to defeat us. We — YOU — must prevent that. Prevent it at all costs. It will require all of your guile — all of your powers of deception."

"At all costs? But how may I stop him? We are not permitted to kill him."

"You must dispirit him. Frighten him into doing as you wish. You must cause him to make the wrong choices for himself and others, eh. By that means, he will divert himself."

"Yes, my lord. I understand. But, you say our interests. What are those, if I may be permitted to know?"

"So, you wish to know what this... this despicable person will do to thwart us, eh?"

"The better to act, my lord," said the shadow, cringing.

There was a silence, as the Evil decided precisely what to convey to his servant. In that silence the shadow quavered and shook with fear.

3

"Well, I suppose it may assist if you know something of my thoughts."

"Yes, my lord. I am certain of it."

"This creature who is coming into your orbit of affairs will launch himself on a path of behavior that will certainly disrupt my allies among the people — the humans. If not deterred, he will be able to assist powerfully those who stand in the way of my allies — in the way of my interests, you see."

"Yes, my lord. He will thwart our allies — those among the humans who are prepared to do our bidding and as you wish."

"Exactly. That is why he must be diverted. Do not fail me, Ozmondura, or you will fade into nothingness and I will have my revenge on <u>you</u>."

The shadow bowed deeply and then backed slowly through the door and into the alley. There he melted into a green mist and disappeared.

CHAPTER THREE
WHEREIN I MEET THE PICKLOCK

1

When I emerged from Reverend Lovecroft's study, my hand still throbbing, I found waiting for me a very fat woman with a large round face that had about three chins. One more than any human is entitled to have, I figured. She told me she was Mrs. Ridley, the matron, all of her chins quivering as she spoke. I learned later that she was also Reverend Lovecroft's sister and her husband, Mr. Ridley, was the Porter of St. Cuthbert's. That meant he was the main jailer.

Meeks handed me over and departed without a word. Mrs. Ridley said only, "Follow me," in a menacing voice, and as she waddled off I followed, down a long passage. Near the end she unlocked the door to a small room — almost a closet — and said, "Wait in here." I entered and sat in the only chair in the room and there I waited, in the dark, all day. Not just an hour or two, but about eight hours. I figured I had arrived at an inconvenient hour and so they decided to store me away for a while. Happily, when I entered I noticed a large can in the corner of the room, which had the stink of a privy.

After hours of sitting in the room, hearing nothing and wondering when I would be released, Mrs. Ridley returned and led me further down the corridor and then into a large room with long tables, where about forty boys, many younger than me, were already eating. They said nothing as we entered and I noticed that no one even looked up. Mr. Ridley, a short thin man with bushy eyebrows enough for three men and small ears, patrolled the room with a rod very much like the one Reverend Lovecroft had used on my hands. I noticed that Mr. Ridley's big flat nose leaned to one side and his bushy eyebrow went clear across his brow without interruption. Still, what you noticed first about Mr. Ridley were his eyes — big, round and sad, like an owl who'd given his last hoot. Soon, he found cause to whack one boy over the back, I guessed because he looked up. I decided not to look up during meals.

"Sit here," said Mr. Ridley, pointing to a space on the bench at the end of one long table. I did so, and in a few minutes, a young girl brought me a bowl of something and a spoon. The something looked very much like porridge, but I could see it had a bone in it. The first taste was about the second worst thing I had ever put in my mouth, close behind a beetle of some sort I had once mistaken for a nut. My first impulse was to spit it out, but something told me that that would bring down Mr. Ridley's rod on my shoulder, so I held it a moment, hoping to get used to it, and then swallowed. I waited for my stomach to send it back up with a rejection notice attached, but when it didn't I suddenly had a great sense of relief. The five spoonfuls of the muck that followed were just as bad, but oddly enough by the end, I was sure I could eat the stuff and keep it down. I was never so proud of my stomach.

All the while we ate I noticed a big grey cat who roamed the dining room relentlessly, apparently hoping to find something to eat. As cats went, this one was an ugly Gawd-help-us — a scruffy, stringy specimen with one gnarly ear and a look in his eyes like he was planning an armed robbery, with violence. If one of the boys happened to drop a morsel on the floor the cat bounded after it and often made quick work before the unlucky boy could retrieve it. I admired his zeal for eating the uneatable. His stomach was stronger than mine. I soon learned that Mr. Ridley did not punish dropping or spitting something on the floor, because the cat cleaned it up quickly and thoroughly.

Finally, Mr. Ridley shouted "All rise!" and everyone stood immediately but remained quiet and motionless, looking down. I dared to make a sidelong glance at the boy next to me — a small skinny lad with curly blond hair and lots of pimples — who I noticed stood with his eyes closed. I decided to do the same.

We stood for a long while until I heard the door open and close and then Reverend Lovecroft's angry dark voice began to utter a prayer of thanksgiving "for the good and bountiful food these sinful urchins have received from you my Lord." I remember thinking that I could not envision my father, who was as saintly as any man I had known, saying such a thing to God.

When the voice finished, the door opened and closed again and Mr. Ridley shouted, "Dismissed to bed!"

With that, all the boys raised their heads and began to file out. I joined the line and followed in silence to a large dormitory, with many cots. Mrs. Ridley, who was somewhere behind us, said "Master St.-John, come this way." I looked round and saw her pointing toward a cot, which I decided was probably where I was to sleep.

"This is your bed, Master St.-John. You will come to it every evening after dinner. Notice how it's dressed. You'll dress it in the same fashion, neatly, every morning when you rise. Do you understand?" she asked in a threatening tone.

"Yes, mum. I do," said I, my eyes down.

I found on the bed, under my pillow, a nightshirt, and noticed that the boys were all undressing and putting on similar garments. I followed, noticing that my nightshirt was too large, by at least a size. No matter, I thought. It might have been too small by three sizes.

While I dressed for bed I noticed that the cat roamed the dormitory, weaving between cots, and apparently searching for mice or rats. He prowled with relentless purpose and somehow it reassured me that he was at work.

As the plugugly cat approached my cot, however, he stopped and looked up at me, quizzically I thought, his head cocked to one side and his eyes narrowed. Then, a voice suddenly came into my mind, which I knew immediately — and I know this sounds strange — I knew it was the voice of the cat.

"What are you looking at, my lad?" he asked, in the accent of a proper English gentleman.

I was imagining this, I knew, and figured it was probably the work of what I had eaten. I dismissed all thought of the cat and turned again to my cot.

In the short time it took everyone to undress and dress, Mr. Ridley shouted, "Lights out!" and in a few seconds we had jumped in the cots and all went dark, except for a dim candle at the far end of the room where there was a can. I lay there, my eyes open, thinking about all that had brought me to this miserable place. And I thought about the pain of that birch rod on the hands, which still smarted for some reason.

As I lay there for a half-hour, thinking I should be so tired that I could sleep, my stomach suddenly leaped and then began to churn strangely. The pride I had felt in the little fellow only an hour earlier began to wane, and I knew I was in for something. What? I did not know.

I lay awake for an hour or more, my stomach churning its disapproval of what it had suffered at dinner. All the while I felt that I might well lose what was in there and yet I was so frightened of the rod and the sure beating I would get that

I worked to hold it down. That only caused more pain and more growling from my stomach. I was sure that others could hear the sound of my groaning and growling.

After a while, things began to calm down and I started to think that I might even be able to sleep. That's when I heard a faint noise from the cot across from my own, and casting an eye into the darkness, I thought I saw a movement. I figured at first it must be the cat or possibly someone going to the chamber pot. I looked more intently and heard another noise, now coming from the direction of the door. It was a low clicking sound that I could hear only because I was right next to the door, but I could not see what was making it.

After about a minute of clicking, I saw the door open a little, admitting a faint light from the passage. A small figure crawled through the door and closed it quickly behind. Then, only silence. I was amazed at whoever opened the door so quickly because I knew Mr. Bailey had locked it when he left.

Instantly, I decided to follow. No concern about the rod or my stomach bothered my brain at all. I was suddenly on the floor crawling to the door, opened it as the figure had done and crawled through, closing it behind me.

2

In the passage, I looked both ways and to the right saw something disappear into the far door. I followed, and when I reached the door I paused, thinking I might find a painful surprise on the other side. A knock on the head, maybe, or a rod across the neck, if it proved to be Reverend Lovecroft.

I opened it slowly and as silently as I could, and yet the hinges squeaked. I could only hope that whoever was on the other side had moved on far enough not to hear me.

Beyond the door, I found a storage room, lighted dimly by a gaslight coming from outside, just as the passage was lighted. It seemed that no one was there, so I crawled to the nearest door, which was open and gave access to another short passage. Now, I crawled slowly down that passage to what looked like another dark room with an open door.

At the door I peered in from about three inches above the floor and saw a short figure standing, back to me, about five feet away. He had something in his hands, which I could not quite make out. He seemed shorter than me, so I dared to stand and enter.

Startled, he began to juggle whatever it was in his hands and almost dropped it, but caught it just in time. I only heard him say, "Coo!" in a low voice. When I drew closer I recognized him as the small boy I'd noticed in the dining room, giving me a sidelong glance as I looked at him. Almost at the same time, I became aware of the odor of the room — a pleasant smell, of food.

"Who are you?" I finally said, in a commanding way.

"I'm Arthur," he replied, looking down at the bowl in his hands.

"What's that you have there and what's this place?" I demanded.

He paused. "Pudding I think. Tastes like cherry pudding. This is the larder."

"Pudding!" I repeated, mouth agape.

He sensed my confusion. "This is where they keep the food for the Muck-mucks. You know, the ones who run the place. Lovecroft and the Baileys and others. They eat a lot better than we do."

"Sure do," I agreed, sniffing and looking around. I didn't wait to take a handful of what was in the bowl and stick it in my mouth. It was delightful. The best pudding I'd ever tasted, I thought.

"I come here often," said Arthur, a hesitant tone in his voice, as if he didn't quite want to let me in on his secret. "But don't eat too much or they'll know I was here. And only take food from the plates that are leftovers. They don't notice that as much, I figure."

"I see," said I, taking up a plate of scraps from the nearby table. When I put it in my mouth, it tasted of lamb stew — something I'd not had in a long while.

Immediately, my curiosity turned to Arthur's ability to open the locked door.

"How'd you open that door?" I asked, frowning and licking my hands. Again he hesitated and looked down.

"Picked the lock," he finally said. "I'm a pick-lock."

"A what?"

"Yes, and I'm darn good at it too," he insisted, more bravely and as if I had doubted him unjustly.

"I could see that," I assured him. "You made quick work of it and I was surprised. Thought you must have a key."

"A key? Right," he scoffed. "Bailey never leaves a key anywhere. He has his keys chained to his trousers. He would leave his trousers behind if he left a key," he gave a faint laugh. "I don't need a key. There's not a lock I can't pick. Hasn't been made."

I smiled to think of it. "I see what you mean."

"I'm a darn good pickpocket too, but not as good as my lock work. That's my trade," he said, giving his chin a proud lift.

"Whose pocket have you picked?"

"I pick Mr. Bailey's all the time. He sometimes has snuff. He's a dipper, you know."

"No, I didn't know that. Just arrived myself, as you've seen, but interesting to know about Bailey."

He looked at me as if to ask a question, but then said nothing.

Not wanting to waste time talking, I turned to the food and began to help myself to more from the plates of unfinished meals. There was plenty wasted and it was as good as any meal I'd ever had. Just as I'd had enough, Arthur warned, "No time to eat more. We must be back. Lingering in here will only get us caught. Mr. Bailey sometimes roams about at night. He's unpredictable. Almost caught me in here once or twice."

No sooner had he spoken than we heard the sound of a distant door and then footsteps in the passage. "This way," Arthur whispered, taking my arm, diving into the recess under a nearby counter, covered by a curtain. I suddenly found myself on top of him, and hardly able to squeeze into the hole, but we both stopped breathing and made no sound at all.

3

Then a lantern's light flashed in the larder. My heart jumped into my throat and stayed there until the light moved on. When I heard Arthur breathe I did the same. We both lay motionless for some time, not wanting to hear the sound of feet shuffling in our direction. Instead, we heard a distant door open and close.

"Gone," said Arthur. "Now you can roll off me and I'll be able to breathe again."

Just outside the larder we found no sign of Mr. Bailey, but I jolted and rocked back to see the cat, looking quizzically at us, as if to ask, "What are you two doing here?"

We stopped momentarily. "What's the cat's name?" I whispered.

"No name. Just The Cat," said Arthur. "Showed-up about a week ago and quickly got the run of the place. Seems to look at everyone with superior disdain, but he does a good job keeping down the mouse population."

"He was in the dormitory before I followed you, so he must have come out with me and trailed me."

"No use for cats, myself. Nasty creatures. Always eating disgusting things. Cause disease too, I've heard, and of course they'll scratch you. So, look out for him."

I didn't agree with Arthur's attitude about cats. I had always liked them. But something about the way this cat looked at Arthur told me the feelings were mutual.

We scurried down to the dormitory door, which was unlocked. Arthur used his skills to relock it and then moved quietly to his cot. I found mine first and fell into a sound sleep, my stomach celebrating my good fortune.

CHAPTER FOUR
WHEREIN COSMO WARNS, "THERE BE DEMONS"

1

The Baileys stormed into the dormitory the next morning at 5 o'clock, screaming that we "urchins" must wake up. When we'd scrambled out of our cots, dressed them, and then ourselves, the Baileys marched us to the dining room where we ate whatever was left over from last evening. The same gruel it seemed, only cold and again; with something in it that had legs. When we stood after breakfast and Reverend Lovecroft came to offer his usual prayer, the Baileys assigned the boys their chores for the day. Two-by-two they ordered us to work, mostly washing something. Because I sat at the end of the table next to Arthur, we were always given our chores together. We became an accidental team. That day — my first day of labor in St. Cuthbert's — the Baileys put us to washing walls in the dining room itself. With scrub brushes, soapy water, and a short ladder, we began our work, and after the scullery girls had cleared the dishes, we found ourselves alone in the giant room.

That's when Arthur started explaining to me about how he picked locks. He had brought his little tools, so he was able to show me the tool he was speaking about at any time. At first, his explanations seemed complicated because I had trouble visualizing the parts of the inner lock he was talking about, but soon, when I had had a chance to look into a lock or two myself, I caught on. Arthur said I was a quick study. "Even quicker than me," he said, a little surprised.

After a week of daily tutoring, during which we washed floors, walls, walkways, furniture, and even cleaned in the Baileys' rooms, Arthur said I had learned all there was to know, "without actually working on locks. You're ready to work on a lock," he smiled. I looked forward to that challenge.

Just then we heard a curious noise and turned to see that it was The Cat, who somehow had found his way into the room or had been there all along. I had noticed him almost every day and I'd begun to sense he was following me for some reason. What unnerved me a little, he just sat there, staring at us in his hard-bitten way, as if listening to everything said between us. For some reason I sensed also that Arthur's dislike for The Cat was personal, somehow, not just a matter of not liking cats. He never explained why, and I finally figured it was probably The Cat's appearance, which was enough to frighten the most hardened criminal. It was mainly the left ear that had somehow been reduced to a mere stub. Still, as we continued our work and he continued to observe, I had no repetition of my hallucination that he could talk to me.

It wasn't easy to find a locked lock that we could work on without being noticed. However, a nice opportunity came when we found ourselves alone, washing walls in a small room where there was a locked closet. From that room, we could easily hear anyone approaching in the outside passage and so we were safe to do some practical study. Looking at the lock, Arthur explained what it was like inside and how he would use the tools. As he used the little tools I observed. Suddenly, all his instruction made perfect sense to me and as he worked, I participated in each move to open the lock. Arthur soon opened it and it amazed me to think that I knew exactly how he'd done it.

Of course, I was eager to try it myself, so Arthur used his tools to re-lock the door and I went to work. Arthur watched and advised as I used the tools. "You are doing very well," he encouraged. "Like you were born to it."

It took me longer than Arthur to do every part of the opening operation, but I persisted, even when I had made a wrong move. Eventually, in about twice the time it had taken Arthur, I opened the door. He smiled. I smiled. But more importantly, I had a great feeling of triumph. I had picked my first lock.

"Congratulations," said Arthur, taking my hand. "You are now a pick-lock." We both continued to smile for some time. Then he challenged. "Alright. Now, lock it."

I had not thought of doing that, but I reasoned that if I could pick a lock I could unpick it, so to speak. Again under Arthur's critical eye and in less time than it had taken me to pick the lock, I locked the door. We smile again and again Arthur congratulated me.

"You are on your way, Percy. Practice will make you an expert in no time, and I can already see that you have a natural talent for this sort of thing. I know these things because I am a natural-born pick-lock myself."

Free to do so, we worked the lock several more times, and each time I got quicker at opening it. Then, we felt compelled to return to our wall washing, but as we worked, Arthur explained to me how some locks differed from the one we'd just worked. I listened intently, wanting to learn every snippet of his experienced wisdom.

That night, as I lay in my cot, I relived in my mind everything that had happened as we worked on that lock — every little piece of the puzzle that every lock truly is. By this means, I retaught myself every night the things I had learned that day, and by my reasoning, I got at least twice the value from Arthur's knowledge and instruction.

2

One night, a week later, I awakened suddenly for no apparent reason, but as I looked over the edge of my cot I gasped to see The Cat, looking up at me with his usual blood-chilling expression. Though there was but the usual dim light in the dormitory, somehow the creature sat in a glowing light that seemed to belong to him alone. I decided to ignore him. I rolled over on my back and quickly fell into a dreamless sleep.

I don't know how long I slept, before something landed on top of me. It took me a few seconds to realize that it was The Cat, who seemed to want to talk, or I supposed I should say, *communicate*.

"Wake up," he demanded, now standing on my chest.

"I'm awake. How could I not be awake with you pouncing on me? What'd y'want now?"

"I must advise you —," he said before I could cut him short. "Listen, Percy. You are headed for big trouble. This lock-picking enthusiasm of yours will only lead to great danger and perhaps even to your demise, my lad. Put an end to it, and think about another line of work altogether. Boot polishing, for example. Plenty of work for boot-polishers out there and might even lead to a good trade as a cobbler, eh?"

By now I was a little annoyed by The Cat's ability to play with my mind, or rather with what I still perceived as my own tendency to play tricks on myself by pretending The Cat's conversation. The more I did so, the more worried I became about my sanity. I figured my grandfather was probably a little potty, so maybe I'd inherited something from the old blister.

"Listen, I don't need your advice about anything because you are a figment of my imagination playing tricks on my own mind."

"What rot!" he scoffed, clearly annoyed at being declared a 'figment'. "I am as real as you are — moreso in fact — and I am only trying to help."

"Alright, if you're not a figment and are trying to help, I have only one question for you. Why? Why do you want to spend time helping me that you could be devoting to catching mice or some other delicacy?"

"Well, if you must know, it's my job to help and guide, and not to catch mice as you say with your gratuitous and hurtful sarcasm."

"Your job? What?"

"Let me explain so that even someone with your limited imagination can understand. I am your Guardian Angel and it is my profession to help. It is your job to sit up and listen and do as I suggest. Then all will be well between Heaven and Earth."

I was just a little knocked back on my heels at this last, because it did not seem to me that even having fun creating imaginings I would come up with something as strange as all that. Of course, I believed in Guardian Angels, but the notion that mine would be a scruffy Gawd-help-us cat with a bad attitude gave me a whack in the middle of the forehead.

"How did I get a Guardian Angel like you? I don't mean to be unkind, but you don't seem like the sort of Guardian Angel I would choose and I am wondering what I did to get you. And, by the way, aren't you supposed to be a tall handsome creature with golden hair, blue eyes and wings that stretch out about ten feet? How'd you end up being a scruffy plugugly?"

He dropped a disappointing look in my direction, in so far as a cat can do so, and then explained.

"It happened because I got myself in a bit of a mess."

"Mess?" I repeated, a little surprised he would say that he was in a mess.

"Being an ugly cat, I mean. And I've only been your GA for about a month. Your previous GA got reassigned and so was I. Neither of us were having much success, but I was reassigned for screwing-up."

"Screwing-up? What does that mean?"

"That's a guardian angel word for making a dashed mess of things and so the leadership finally gave me the push. Got yanked from my assignment and stuck to you, where I have a chance to redeem myself. I don't mind telling you if I screw this up, I don't know where I could be sent. Being your GA is about the bottom of the profession, if you'll pardon me for saying so."

I didn't like the sound of that but all the business about making a mess of things jolted my curiosity, so I decided to pry deeper into The Cat's disappointing history.

"Who'd you make a mess of?" I asked, now curious to know his sordid story. His eyes narrowed and then he looked away, as if too embarrassed to continue.

"My previous person was Wilhelm von Hohenzollern."

"What!" I said, falling back into the cot. "You were guardian angel to the German Emperor!"

"Yes I'm afraid so," he sighed. "I admit it."

"Well, I can see what you mean by 'screwed-up'. If there's a messier soul in Europe than the German Kaiser's I can't imagine who it belongs to."

He shook his head. "Yes, lad, that was my one chance to make the big team in the guardian angel business and I made a pig's breakfast of it. Now I'm back where I started. But, the Kaiser's soul is not for me to judge," he replied. "My concern now is with yours, eh?"

"If what you claim is true, I suppose I must know your name. Not 'The Cat' is it?"

"No," he said. "My name is Cosmo."

Now, as suddenly as he had come, Cosmo wandered off, leaving me to lay awake for about an hour wondering why I was having such vivid imaginings about guardian angels who looked like a shopworn cat with bad indigestion. I decided it was probably because the whole atmosphere of St. Cuthbert's made me feel threatened — especially by painful birch rods — and it was reassuring to think I might have a bit of protection. Finally, I concluded I had more important things to consider than my fantasy about guardian angels. I fell into a deep sleep that only ended when Mr. Bailey shouted; "Wake up!" in my ear.

3

In the coming weeks, Arthur and I found opportunities to practice on various kinds and brands of locks, and in those weeks I had no more 'conversations' with Cosmo. I decided to say nothing about Cosmo to anyone — even Arthur — lest I get sent from St. Cuthbert's Asylum to an insane asylum.

As we worked together, I found myself interested to learn Arthur's history — how he'd ended up at St. Cuthbert's. When I asked questions, however, it was clear he didn't want to talk about it, even so far as to tell me his last name. I guessed that it was just too painful for him, so I soon let it go.

One day Arthur asked if I would also like to learn the pickpocket's trade. While I was not nearly as attracted to that as to locks, I said I would. It was then that my education as a pickpocket began in earnest. Both Arthur and I wore jackets with inside and outside pockets, and so there was plenty of real-life picking to be done on each other. I learned first that there are two things needed for success — distraction and a light touch — but there are many ways to pick a pocket and many ways needed depending on the pocket being picked.

Arthur advised me on the few things that every beginning pickpocket should know. "Many people," he said, "believe that a buttoned pocket is a protection against being picked. Not at all. While a buttoned pocket is a bit more difficult, it's an easy matter. All part of the process of picking, and you need to be prepared to find a pocket buttoned. Assume it, alright?"

"Right."

"Also, a purse is much easier to pick than a pocket, so prefer women over men, and especially a woman who has a big purse on her forearm. It's like she's offering it to you to pick."

"Right," I said.

"And third, most men carry their coin purse in their waistcoat pocket and their wallet in the inside pocket of their jacket or coat. Don't bother to pick the pockets of working men. They have no money and besides, they could not afford to lose it."

"Right."

"Those are the main dos and don'ts of the trade. There are others I'll tell you about as we go along, but they can wait. Now, we must start your practical learning."

"Good. I like that."

Thereafter Arthur gave me the sage advice that every fledgling pickpocket receives from his teacher. "Front pockets are much harder to pick than back. We are short, so we have a special disadvantage in going for a man's interior coat pocket."

"I see. Makes sense to me."

"And never forget, the success of a pickpocket depends as much on distraction as on the lightness of touch. Become a master at distraction and it will increase your chances of success a hundredfold."

"But how do you distract?"

"Don't worry about that. I'll teach you plenty about distraction in the coming weeks."

Arthur was so sure of his ability to teach what he called "the art of distraction" that I was confident immediately. And in the coming weeks, he made good his promise. I learned that distraction is much easier if you work in twos — one to distract and one to pick. But even alone, bumping and dropping things in front of someone are two good ways. It also helps to follow someone until they distract themselves. "Everyone does," advised Arthur, "about every twenty minutes on the street. Just follow and be patient. Patience is a good virtue for a pickpocket."

"I see. I have that one for sure. The patience of an oyster."

"Good. You'll need it in the trade."

"One other thing about distraction. It helps to have the assistance of a pretty girl as your distractor. Men are more than willing to be distracted by a pretty face, especially if it is doing something interesting right in front of them."

I hadn't thought of that myself, but it was obviously true. Arthur's insights into things about human behavior were remarkable to me, and I soaked them up like a bath sponge.

At first, I practiced on Arthur himself, who was keen to tell me when my touch was too heavy and to observe when it improved and ultimately when it was "perfect."

"Now," he said one spring morning, "you are ready to practice your skill on one of the boys. They'll make good practice I figure."

I knew instantly he was right.

In contrast to all of his admirable qualities, there was one thing about Arthur that you couldn't miss. He was frail. As I worked with him I noticed he always appeared tired, even just after a night's sleep and he often cleared his throat or coughed quietly. At first, I thought it was just a mannerism, but as I observed him more closely and got to know him, I realized there was something amiss with Arthur. He was ill. The only good thing was that he never seemed to get worse, and he never complained.

In the following days, Arthur insisted that I was ready to try my pocket-picking skills on unsuspecting "victims". He chose for my first try a boy named Willard — a long willowy lad with hair like a Raggedy Ann doll and a back pocket that was always stuffed with something. He was the perfect "victim." My first try at his pocket was a miss and it seemed that he felt my touch. He turned suddenly to look down into my face, angrily I thought. Arthur said he merely heard me close behind him and reacted badly, but I wasn't so sure. I waited several hours to make my next try at Willard and this time I succeeded. As he walked away from me going the other way I snatched a small envelope from his pocket and continued walking. Arthur, who watched the action, said it was "flawless."

Later I returned the envelope to Willard, saying I'd seen it fall from his pocket as he walked down the passage toward the dormitory.

The next day, Arthur chose a harder victim for me — a small boy named Martin. He was a fidgety sort of fellow who seemed very athletic and invariably walked quickly. Seemed to never stand still. Figuring out how to pick his pocket was a torment, but I finally got good at it. After a week or two, he started getting suspicious of why I was always returning things he'd dropped from his pocket, so I decided to find another victim. Still, I considered it a great achievement that I'd learned to empty Martin's pocket regularly.

The only exception to success at picking pockets came shortly after Martin and it was a result of my strange imaginings. Further evidence that something was wrong in my mind.

I decided on my own to pick the pocket of a boy named Rupert — a close friend of Arthur's. He was one of the older lads and though quiet seemed to me to be very intelligent. I figured he would be a good challenge and I was right.

I followed him one day with an eye toward emptying his pocket and every time I thought was right to try, he made an unexpected move of some sort that defeated me. It seemed to me almost uncanny how he evaded my best efforts. Then one morning I saw him speaking to Arthur in the corridor as boys passed them going both ways. I came up behind Rupert and made my try for his back pocket. Suddenly, however, a hand grabbed my wrist in a painful grip. Immediately I saw that it was no ordinary hand that had me, but rather a claw of dark green with only three "fingers" — each with a long sharp nail. Even in my pain it struck me immediately as odd that the hand seemed to come from Rupert's back pocket — not one of his hands at all, but another. Even with that, somehow the strangest part of the thing was that while Rupert's ugly green hand held my wrist in agony, he and Arthur continued talking in the most ordinary way and neither of them seemed to notice that I was standing behind Rupert, bleating like a sheep with a painful past.

Just then, Rupert released my hand. I didn't wait to be seized again in the painful grip. I moved along quickly down the passage, holding my hand and still trying not to let out a scream.

All that day I remained in a kind of shock at what had happened. Later, I was able to ask Arthur about his conversation with Rupert, to find out if he had noticed anything strange.

"How could I notice anything?" he asked. "I haven't talked to Rupert at all today."

Hearing this caused me to give a little at the knees. That confirmed my fear. My hallucinations had now taken on a strange and more frightening dimension. I never knew when one of them would suddenly give me a painful jolt. It also seemed unreal because, despite the painful grip, my hand felt fine.

Meanwhile, sad experience as a pickpocket eventually prompted me to return to my preferred "trade" as a picklock. I resumed my nighttime practice on locks throughout the Asylum, most importantly locks that were stronger and newer. Those were invariably on doors that the Baileys and Reverend wanted to remain safely locked. The larder was a hard lock, but so were the locks to other storerooms. The pantry, where mostly bulk supplies and canned goods were kept was tough, but I mastered it sooner than I expected.

One night, as I opened a storeroom with a tough new lock, I found Cosmo inside, looking at me in his cockeyed way and as before, all aglow. My heart sank that I was once again having hallucinations, especially because I knew there was no way Cosmo could be in a locked storeroom.

"Good-day, m'lad!" he said with the usual cheerful lilt in his voice.

"Why do you talk like that? Like a lord in Parliament?" I asked. He took offense and frowned.

"None of my doing, lad. Nor was it my choice to be a hard-luck cat, when in truth I am a proper gentleman. It all came with my reassignment. Just between us, I think someone in the GA leadership has it in for me, but that's another matter."

"So, why are you here now?" I wanted to ask, "What have I done to deserve another visit from you?" But I decided to be civil instead.

"I must intervene, my lad, to warn you against this pocket-picking aspiration of yours. I know you believe you are learning it with the best of intentions, but there's trouble in it for both of us. You will be much happier learning a good trade, like boot making or grocery vending. You will be safer that way, as I have told you in the past."

"And you'll be sure to get that promotion, eh?"

He did not reply. No use disputing with him, I figured, so I let it go and then decided on a new approach — that something might be learned about one figment of my imagination by asking another figment of my imagination.

"Did you see what happened when I tried to pick Rupert's pocket?"

Cosmo looked side-to-side, as if to make sure no one was listening to our thoughts.

"Yes indeed, laddie. The whole nightmare. Quite a shock, I must say."

"And what *was* that? Was it real?"

He glanced to his left again. His eyes narrowed and he leaned toward me.

"There be demons in this place," he said in a confidential whisper. "More demons than just young Rupert, eh."

Just then I thought I heard a distant sound behind me. I turned, and when I looked back Cosmo was gone. And yet, in my mind I heard him say again, "Aye, there be demons in this place."

CHAPTER FIVE
WHEREIN I HAVE DANGEROUS AMBITIONS

1

Despite Cosmo's warning, it was not long before my ambitions as a picklock blossomed and I began to think what would be the hardest lock in the Asylum to pick. There seemed no doubt it would be the lock to Reverend Lovecroft's study. If anyone could afford the best lock in the world and probably had bought it, surely it was Reverend Lovecroft.

My sense of danger told me to resist trying to open that lock, or to even go near it, but as is usually the case with me, the war between fear and ambition was no contest. I began to plan how I could get myself to Lovecroft's lock and open it. I supposed that Mr. Bailey would be no problem, because he likely did not even bother to check the doors to that part of St. Cuthbert's during his nightly watch duties, probably because he was lazy and assumed no one would succeed in getting in there, anyway. The locks were too good, eh?

That was enough to convince me that the only locks to satisfy my growing skill as a picklock were the ones surrounding Reverend Lovecroft's study. As it turned out there were three. One to enter a short passage that led to the anteroom of his study. One to get in there. And then one to get in the study itself. I didn't think Bailey had the keys to any of those locks because Reverend Lovecroft probably did not trust him with them. The Reverend Lovecroft did not strike me as a man to trust anyone, even his own sister and brother-in-law. So, after getting past the first lock, I figured I would be pretty safe.

2

Three nights later and still determined to take on the toughest locks, I awakened suddenly to find Cosmo standing on my chest, with his eyes glowing in the dim light of the dormitory.

"I know what you've decided lad and I am here to warn you. It can only lead to trouble."

"If you know something I don't, what trouble are you talking about? Or, rather, thinking about?"

"The kind of trouble that'll land you in a far worse place than St. Cuthbert's. That's what," he said, narrowing his glowing eyes to an evil squint. Then his mouth seemed to curl up in a knowing smile. I don't mind telling you that seeing Cosmo smile was unnerving.

"Of course, there is some benefit to be had from your recklessness, but —."

He cut himself short, then continued, "But I'll not say more, lest you cause me to screw-up again and I end up as GA to a swamp slug in the Amazon."

Putting aside the curious issue of whether or not Amazon swamp slugs have guardian angels, I asked, "What do you mean 'possible benefit'?" I demanded, just a little indignant that he seemed to think me an incompetent and the suggestion that being my guardian angel was just one step above being guardian angel to a swamp slug in the Amazon.

"Well, m'lad. I know things, eh? From wandering about the place and observing and you can take my guardian angel word for it that Lovecroft's a bad one. But, that's the thing, don't you see. You are not prepared to go head-to-head with such a fiend — believe me."

I could see that Cosmo was not willing to tell more about Reverend Lovecroft, but somehow his warning encouraged rather than deterred me.

Early next morning I rose and quietly moved through the dark passages of the Asylum, to where I remembered the study was. I quickly found the passage door and by the light of a small candle, I went to work on it with Arthur's little tools, keeping an ear open for any footsteps that would signal Mr. Bailey's approach. I worked quickly but precisely and sure enough, the lock was new and tougher than any I had tried yet. It was a German lock, from the label on it, and well-made. I worked a long while, almost despairing that I could open it, but then a click of success and the knob turned. I was in, trying all the while to remember what had finally worked. I reversed that and re-locked the door on the first try. *Those Germans are tricky devils*, I mused to myself as I turned to the next door.

When I reached the second lock my heart sank to see that it was different and obviously new. I cursed a little and then went to work, not wanting to waste time fretting. The lock, though new, was English and it proved easier to open. I was just more familiar with the way the English made locks and it showed in my ease of dealing with it. In only a minute I was in the anteroom with the door locked behind me.

Candle held high I turned to face what I suspected would be the toughest lock of all and I wasn't disappointed. Reverend Lovecroft had spared no expense in securing his study. It had two locks — one ordinary lock at the knob and a deadbolt above that. I worked first on the lower lock and struggled mightily with it for a full five minutes. It was hard to figure out and though I couldn't tell I thought it must be a foreign lock of some kind. Eventually, I figured it out and heard a reassuring click. Then I went to work on the deadbolt. It was easier to work and in only a few more minutes I opened the door to Reverend Lovecroft's inner sanctum.

At first, I thought about relocking it and retreating quickly. After all, I had come to test my skills on the toughest locks in the Asylum and I had mastered them. Good work for one night. But then I reckoned that I had come so far and had worked so hard, I ought to go into the study and take a look around.

I don't know why, but my excitement at opening the locks gave way to a creepy feeling, as I entered the study. I felt the awful sensation of a parade of cockroaches marching up and down my spine. Maybe because that was where I'd gotten the painful whack on the hands with the rod. But then, something rocked me back on my heels and caused my heart to jump into my throat where it started bouncing off my tonsils. There, inside the study sat Cosmo, square in the middle of Reverend Lovecroft's desk, his eyes narrow and pointed right at me.

"Well, m'lad, I see you've decided to ignore my excellent advice and here we are."

"Yes," I said, jutting my chin belligerently, "here we are and I picked three gawdawful locks to get here."

"Now you are here and in a willful attitude, perhaps you'll want to prove yourself on that door over there," he said nodding malevolently toward what appeared to be a closet or storage room.

After more glancing around the study, I decided to have a look beyond the new door. Its lock was not difficult and I opened it in only a minute. And to my great surprise, there was only one thing inside — an iron chest with a large antique lock on it. It was clearly where you would store valuables so I immediately said to myself *this is Reverend Lovecroft's treasure chest.*

"You got that one right, laddy," I heard Cosmo say into my mind.

I might have stood there much longer in my wonder, except that I heard the unexpected. Footsteps outside the study door! It was either Mr. Bailey or worse — Reverend Lovecroft. At any rate, I had been wrong about not being disturbed.

The footsteps approached the study door and then the doorknob rattled. I blew out my candle, closed the closet door, and stood in the darkness, breathless. Somehow, being breathless in a sadist's study in dark is about five times more distressing than being breathless in the full light of a spring day in the park. The door rattled again, but then the footsteps retreated. I heard the door to the anteroom close and then the other door.

I breathed again, but my heart was still in my throat, now wrapped around my uvula and hanging on for dear life. I had been so confident that Arthur was right about Mr. Bailey. That he "never checks the Reverend Lovecroft's study." *Right!* I took some consolation that I had remembered to lock all the doors behind me, so Mr. Bailey had found nothing out of the ordinary.

As I finally summoned up the courage to open the study door and then locked it behind me, I had the uneasy feeling that Mr. Bailey might return at any moment. I was spooked and knew the feeling would last at least until I was back in my cot. I opened the first door and crept down the passage, making sure of my silence. I opened the second door, knowing all the while Mr. Bailey was waiting on the other side to nab me, but to my surprise, the outer passage was empty. I moved quickly but silently to the right and toward the dormitory door, which I opened quickly, locked behind me, slid effortlessly into my cot, and pulled up my blanket. It was then I breathed my first complete breath and felt my heart slide back down into my chest. As I drifted to sleep, I thanked God that I had evaded capture, assuming that God had something to do with it. Of course, I knew Cosmo would say I was presuming far too much of Him.

3

The next day, Arthur was so tired that Mrs. Bailey excused him from work. That put me out alone and to my surprise, Mr. Bailey assigned me to go alone to the anteroom outside Reverend Lovecroft's study and wash floors and clean furniture.

I was working at that job as Reverend Lovecroft arrived. I did not look up, but continued cleaning. He saw me, sniffed, and entered his study. I heard no more from him until a short, pare-shaped man with a thin mustache, wearing a long frockcoat and a topper. He looked important — a proper gent — but I'd never seen him. He knocked boldly on the study's door.

"Who is it!" came the angry question from inside.

"Littlejohn," said the fat man, removing his hat.

"Enter."

Littlejohn entered hesitantly I thought, as if he might be attacked. All this made me curious about what was happening inside, so I decided to wash the floor closer to the door.

"How are things at the County Council?" I heard Reverend Lovecroft ask, in a tone that suggested he didn't much care. "Very well, I suppose."

"Oh quite. Collections have never been better."

"You should know, as the Council's accountant, eh?"

"Quite. But the rate collection is not what I've come about."

"What then?" Reverend Lovecroft asked, angrily, it seemed to me.

"You know what about. About our agreement. Have you given some thought to my proposal? It's been more than a month."

"Yes, of course, I have. I don't see why you shouldn't have more, as you say. How much more is, of course, a matter for negotiation."

"I want half. After all, I fix the books so you can make off with half the Asylum's yearly allotment and I want half of that for my services, eh. I deserve at least half for what I do."

There was a long pause. I heard a chair move as if the Reverend has risen from his desk.

"Half's a great deal. I'd not reckoned on that."

"It's the least I'll accept for what I do. Unless I get it, there'll be no more fixing things. That's an end to it."

After another long pause, the Reverend replied. "Alright, I suppose you leave me no alternative but to give you half."

"There's more."

"More? You want more?"

"Not more money. I want an agreement. Between us."

"But we have an agreement already."

"You don't understand. I want a contract. A written agreement."

"What!"

"Yes. I want something I can hang my hat on, so to speak. I'm an accountant. I believe in contracts."

"You want me to sign a written agreement as to what we are doing?" Lovecroft's tone told me he couldn't believe what he was hearing.

"Absolutely. I have two copies in my pocket."

There was another pause, I supposed while Littlejohn took the copies from his pocket and unfolded them on the desk.

"We'll each sign. One copy for you and one for me. That will make everything very tidy. And because both of us sign, you won't need to worry about me being careless with my copy. After all, it implicates me too, eh."

"I won't do it," said the Reverend. "I won't sign anything."

"Then I am afraid, my friend, that our association is at an end. There'll be no more money for you or me and I'll make a strict accounting of what you spend here at the Asylum. Good day to you, sir."

I heard the door handle rattle and so I moved away on the floor.

"No, wait," said Reverend Lovecroft, loud enough for me to hear.

There was another silence, as I crawled back to the door.

"Alright. I'll sign. I suppose you are right. Our collaboration is such that we can both rely upon the other to keep things a secret. What serves the one, serves the other, eh?"

"Absolutely," said Littlejohn, a smile in his voice. "We're in this thing together."

During the silence that followed, I supposed that the Reverend and Littlejohn were signing the documents.

"Here is your copy, then," I heard Littlejohn say, "and now I'll bid you goodday, Reverend Lovecroft."

When I heard that I crawled quickly to the furthest corner of the anteroom.

"Oh yes," said the Reverend a little absentmindedly, "Good-day Littlejohn."

At that, the fat man emerged from the study with a paper in the side pocket of his coat, and without even noticing me departed. When he'd closed the anteroom door behind him and made his way down the short passage, I heard a door open inside the study. I figured the Reverend had opened the closet. A rattling sound told me he was opening his big chest. Right away I knew that the Reverend was tucking his contract with Littlejohn in the safety of his iron chest.

Though I continued to wash the floor for a few more minutes, it seemed to me that I did not want the Reverend to find me in the anteroom. He would be far too suspicious that I'd overheard his chat with Littlejohn. I left early, deciding to risk Mr. Bailey's anger.

"Why are you back so early?" he asked.

"Oh, Reverend Lovecroft had a visitor and I figured he'd not want me outside his door, where I could hear what was said."

Bailey scrunched up his big crooked nose and frowned.

"Aye, I suppose that's so, right enough."

CHAPTER SIX
WHEREIN MY LIFE IS CHANGED BY ANOTHER TRAGEDY

1

Arthur seemed fine the next day, but as we worked and talked in the coming days I noticed a change. He was slower and seemed preoccupied. He coughed more too and cleared his throat more often. At first, I gave it no concern, but then I decided to ask.

"Oh, sometimes my little cough gets worse and I feel more tired, but then it gets better and I feel fine. No worry," he said.

I took his word for it but continued to watch him more closely. It did not seem to me his cough was getting better and it even appeared to be getting worse. He was more fatigued too and so, despite his assurance, I began to worry more about him.

My fretting increased when one night I awakened at midnight. I don't know why, but I looked across to Arthur's cot, where I saw a small, faint glowing green ball hovering just above Arthur's head. It disappeared almost as soon as I noticed it, and so I knew it was there because of my worry about him. My mind was telling me that something evil was hovering over his life.

Next morning, just after we got to a small storeroom where we were washing shelves, Arthur suddenly erupted in a terrible cough and then spit up blood on the floor. The sight of Arthur's blood shook me, though at first I couldn't believe it. Blood! When he'd finished, he looked up at me as if to say, 'I am feeling terrible', but he was too tired to speak. I quickly took hold of him and with one arm draped round my neck, I helped him the short distance down the passage to the dormitory, where he fell into his cot, curled up, and began to cough even more violently. No blood this time, however.

I ran for Mrs. Bailey, thinking she'd know what to do. When I entered the kitchen shouting, "Arthur is sick!" she threw down the towel she was using and followed me down the passage to Arthur's cot. When we arrived, he was on his back, still coughing violently and struggling for breath. He sucked in breath with a gasp, but his gasping was not getting the job done.

When I looked at Mrs. Bailey — her eyes filled with fright — she looked around, seeming not to know what to do, but probably looking for Mr. Bailey. She dashed — well, waddled quickly — out into the passage, yelling at the top of her lungs for her husband.

When Mr. Bailey arrived, panting and frowning, he put his hand to Arthur's forehead, looked him over, listened to his labored breathing for a bit, and then said, "Nothing terribly wrong here. Leave the boy in bed to rest and he'll be better by morning. No worry."

The same thing that Arthur had said. "No worry." Only now I was very worried and I could tell that Mrs. Bailey was also. As Mr. Bailey led her away by the forearm, she looked back at Arthur, with fear written all over her face.

2

I listened to Arthur most of the night. Not much sleep for either of us. He mostly coughed, but sometimes I heard him gasping for air. By morning he was noticeably worse. Gurgling, gasping, and more uncomfortable. When Mr. Bailey arrived, I told him about Arthur's night. Mrs. Bailey arrived just after, still clearly distressed. Both stood over Arthur's cot, staring at him as he struggled for air.

"Davy, go get the Reverend," said Mrs. Bailey, pointing to the door. Mr. Bailey ran out, doing as he was told. While he was gone and after the boys filed out to their work, I decided to press my case with Mrs. Bailey, who was now wringing her hands as she looked down in distress.

"He needs a doctor, don't you think?"

She looked at me but said nothing. I said it again, with even more conviction.

"I think he needs a doctor. He's getting no air. He'll die soon!"

She continued to look at Arthur with a frightful glare, but still said nothing. Just then, Reverend Lovecroft arrived, a handkerchief over his mouth and nose, followed by Mr. Bailey. Mrs. Bailey looked up and explained, as the Reverend stood over the cot.

"Been this way since yesterday. Gasping and Heaven knows what else. He's even spit up some blood, this boy says," she moaned, looking at me. The Reverend didn't look up, but stood a long minute, gazing at Arthur. Mrs. Bailey repeated her opinion.

"Seems the boy needs a doctor, eh? He's in a bad way."

"Nonsense!" Reverend Lovecroft finally scoffed. "D'ye think we can pay a doctor at the slightest sniffles, woman? He has the *rheum* (a cold). That's all. Give him a bit of sulfur and a spoon of Mr. Gilford's Magic Elixir and he'll be fine in the morning. No doubt."

Mrs. Bailey did not seem reassured but raised no objection. As Reverend Lovecroft turned and left, Mr. Bailey went for the sulfur and elixir. He returned in a few minutes and as Mrs. Bailey held up Arthur's head, Mr. Bailey spooned first the sulfur and then the magic elixir into Arthur's mouth. He coughed and struggled a little, but in a minute or two, he fell into a deep sleep. I hoped that somehow the medicine would do its work.

I listened through most of the night and heard Arthur cough only a little. I was reassured. In the morning he opened his eyes, and he seemed much improved. I spoke to him and he understood what I was saying, but remained too weak to reply. Still, I was delighted at his improvement. Arthur remained in his cot all that day and the next, only rising to use the chamber pot and to take a bit of soup that Mrs. Bailey brought. He seemed to be recovering. We saw no more of the Reverend, nor of Mr. Bailey, except at those times Mr. Bailey came to wake us and put us to work. I worked alone, thinking all the while of Arthur and hoping his recovery would continue.

Just as my optimism was soring I heard a snort. It was one of those epic snorts like a hippopotamus with nasal congestion. It was Cosmo, staring up at me from beside Arthur's cot.

"Listen, m'lad," he warned. "Arthur is not improving and it's time you do something to get help for him."

"Like what? You heard Reverend Lovecroft. He refuses to call a doctor. What can I do?" I asked, hoping for some angelic insights or suggestions. Just shows you how desperate I was that I was looking to my own hallucinations for advice. If anyone ever asks you how dumb Percy St.-John can be, well there you have it.

"I don't know," said Cosmo, "but it must be something big. Only a big something is going to get Arthur his one chance."

"Something big, eh?" *Well that's as useful as teats on a boar hog,* I thought. *I know no more now than before Cosmo popped-up.*

3

Now yet another buzz overtook the Asylum — the approach of the Christmas Season. All the boys knew that at Christmas well-wishing people donated presents and there was a general distribution of useful things. Gifts like cakes, sugar cubes soaked in rum, bars of soap, and even clothing—mostly castoffs like old caps and coats. During the Christmas Season, the County Council members and their wives and children also made an annual visit to the Asylum, and they usually brought gifts as well. Mr. Bailey and his wife greeted the coming of the Councilmen with great distress; it seemed to me, eager to ensure that all was tidy and clean and fearful that something amiss would be noticed and they'd be blamed.

They, therefore, put us to work even more energetically, standing over us and inspecting our work more closely. We got more whacks of the rod too. Everything had to be clean and now that meant sparkling clean. Arthur returned to work in a few days, but he was constantly tired and clearly not recovered. I began to worry that he would soon decline again. My fears came true even sooner than I expected. In a few days, he began to cough more and to fail. When we took to our cots that night Arthur was breathing heavily and soon he was gasping. I rose from my cot and knelt beside Arthur, only able to see his face in the dim light of the distant lantern.

"Percy," he said faintly. "Percy."

"Yes. I'm here," I whispered.

Now his speech fell to a barely audible whisper.

"Good-bye, Percy. Good... ."

His voice trailed off just as I was about to shake him and ask him what the hell he was saying by 'Good-bye'." Then I noticed it. He was no longer struggling for breath ... no longer breathing at all. I started beating on his chest, but nothing. I took his hand and massaged it, I don't know why. But nothing.

It was then I was seized by a real sense of panic. I ran for the door to find Mrs. Bailey. Pounding at the Baileys' door, it was not difficult to rouse them. Both opened it and responded quickly to my plea that Arthur was dying.

Mr. Bailey scurried off to find Reverend Lovecroft, while Mrs. Bailey waddled ahead of me to the dormitory. As we stood over Arthur in the dim light, we could both see that he had stopped breathing. Mrs. Bailey began to fret audibly, just as Reverend Lovecroft and Mr. Bailey arrived.

"It's the boy, Arthur, again," she said as Lovecroft looked down at the cot. "He not breathing. He's...."

Lovecroft said nothing for what seemed the longest while. Then turning to Mr. Bailey, he whispered, so as not to wake the dormitory.

"Just when the Council are coming. The little blighter couldn't have awaited a day or two."

"Aye."

"No time to dispose of him now. Wrap him in his sheet and put him in the storeroom and put a sign on the door that says Infirmary: Contagious Patient Inside. That'll keep out the prying eyes. After the Council visit, you can bury him out back with the others."

With the others, I thought to myself as I heard this last. *What others?* I might have thought more about this but by now I was motionless with grief. I had trouble breathing. Soon Lovecroft and the Baileys were gone, along with Arthur, and I was left to sit on my cot and weep for Arthur. The one thought that seemed to press on me like a thousand pound weight was that somehow I seemed to be doomed to suffer the loss of everyone who was close to me. Every person I came to love was somehow taken away in an instant. It seemed to me that perhaps I was peculiarly cursed to lose those I loved and that made me even sadder. I could not imagine why.

The night passed slowly in such thoughts. Like the night my father had died. I knew I should be thinking of many other things, but I could only think of Arthur being gone and the additional tragedy that I had failed to save him. In my gloom, I reproached myself that I had failed to save him.

CHAPTER SEVEN
WHEREIN I CAUSE A RIOT

1

Odd, how I think my worst thoughts and do my best work at midnight. At what I reckoned was nearing midnight I began to think of other things — most notably my anger at Lovecroft and the Baileys and how they'd let Arthur die. Without caring. And, how they were hiding their evil from the coming Council Visit. My anger about how Arthur had been treated finally rose to compete with my grief and then I found myself overcome with the determination to do something — anything — about the evil that had been done.

What shook me out of my deadening and almost paralyzing sorrow was the thought that no one but I would see that what had been done to Arthur was set right. Now that the worst had happened, I knew the only thing I could do for Arthur was to get justice for him — somehow.

I'd long since decided to return to the Reverend's study and have a look inside his iron chest. Now, I made up my mind to do so that night. In the meantime, I hatched another plan in my mind — a scheme to avenge Arthur that would be possible only if I found what I expected to discover in that chest.

Once again I waited until I could hear Mr. Bailey finishing his rounds and go to bed. Finally, the deathly silence of everything was my signal to act. Once again, using Arthur's little tools to unlock and re-lock doors behind me, I soon found myself looking at the now-familiar German lock on the Reverend's study door. In the study I placed my candle on a nearby bookcase and by its dim light began to work on the closet lock. I was so nervous that it took three tries to open the door, but once inside I made short work of the ancient lock on the chest. Holding high my candle I opened the chest and, though I had expected something good inside, I was unprepared for what I found. Stacks of banknotes and piles of gold — hundreds of gold sovereigns.

However, there was yet another treasure in the box. A folded paper. When I opened it and read I knew at once it was the document Reverend Lovecroft had signed with Littlejohn. I stuffed it in my pocket. Happily, I had brought an old potato sack with me. I quickly emptied the box of its notes, most of them bound together in 10 and 20-pound packets, and then emptied the gold. I shouldered the sack holding my newfound riches, closed and relocked the chest, did the same with the study doors, and made my way through the passages to the dormitory.

2

It was now that my full plan came flooding into my mind. The Council was due early in the morning, we had all been told, and so I had to work fast to put my scheme into action. I couldn't sleep at all, but that was fine because I needed to get up early to do my work. First, by the light of my little candle, I reached into the bag and counted out a thousand pounds in notes and ten gold sovereigns. I stuffed these in all my pockets, including my coat. I was bulging all over with money. Then, taking my sack of notes and gold, I retraced my steps, not bothering to relock doors behind me. I walked down every dark passage in the Asylum, throwing out notes and gold. When I returned to the dormitory it was almost time for Mr. Bailey to rouse the boys. I tossed out the last of my banknotes and then woke them myself.

"WAKE UP AND GET RICH!" I screamed at the top of my voice. The boys scrambled to their feet and began to dress, and that's when they noticed the banknotes and gold I'd thrown out. When a fierce scramble started, I announced again at the top of my lungs "THERE'S MUCH MORE IN THE PASSAGE!" I flung open the door, just as an astonished Mr. Bailey, his jaw hanging open, was about to enter the dormitory. He was overrun by a wave of boys, all eager to get their share of the treasure scattered in all the passages.

3

Soon, a riot of forty boys and some of the kitchen girls was coursing through the Asylum, screaming and cursing and celebrating the free money. Boys were fighting over gold and Mrs. Bailey, I could see, had joined the *mêlée*, getting her share of the loot. Mr. Bailey too, after a bit, beating boys to hand over their ill-gotten riches. Soon the boys had found cudgels of their own and were beating Mr. Bailey bloody senseless, while the kitchen girls kicked Mrs. Bailey to the floor and relieved her of all the notes she'd managed to stuff into her clothing. In the process the girls tore off Mrs. Bailey's dress. Then the riot somehow seemed even more outrageous, as Mrs. Bailey ran about in her underlinen.

In the passage I also noticed Cosmo, running up and down, yowling and dodging the trampling feet — desperate to find an escape from danger.

As the riot reached its full fury, the bailiff was forced to open the Asylum gates to admit the County Council's carriages and coaches. There were ten at least and as the gentlemen and their families alighted and entered the Asylum, they found not Reverend Lovecroft to welcome them but rather a full-blown stampede of boys and kitchen girls, now joined by a few of the groundskeepers and bailiffs. It was a sight to see, and though I would have enjoyed watching it for a few hours more, I sensed it was time for me to take my loot and bid St. Cuthbert's goodbye. On my way out I encountered several members of the County Council and their wives, just alighting from their coaches. I handed one of them the copy of the "contract" that Mr. Littlejohn had forced the Reverend Lovecroft to sign.

"Here, sir," I said, pushing the document in his face. "You'll want to read this and then share it with other members of the Council. I promise that all of you will find it very interesting."

He took it, with a surprised look. Then I turned to the woman I figured was his wife.

"Mum," I said, bowing, "you'll find the body of a dead boy in the storeroom on the second floor. There are other bodies buried out back. Hidden by Lovecroft."

"What!" she exclaimed, as the others muttered. 'Dead!' 'Buried!'

"Yes. His name was Arthur," I explained. "He died because Lovecroft would not call in a doctor!"

With that, I doffed my cap and made for the gate, where to my relief no bailiff waited to stop me from leaving. I ran as fast as I could down the road and toward the river, where I was sure to find the main road to take me north into central London.

As I ran, a cat dashed across the road in front of me. It resembled Cosmo, I thought, but then I dismissed the notion that he could have escaped ahead of me. In fact, as I walked and ran I was suddenly very pleased to leave my hallucinations behind. Part of the disappearing nightmare of St. Cuthbert's, I told myself. As I made my way down the London road, I considered that this was indeed the unhappiest Christmas I'd ever yet had.

PART TWO
MR. FINERMANN'S SECRET LIFE

CHAPTER EIGHT
WHEREIN I PURSUE UNFINISHED BUSINESS

1

I didn't trust the Council blighters to do right by Arthur. After all, they'd paid so little attention to St. Cuthbert's for years that Lovecroft and Littlejohn had robbed them blind. And, how could they be so blind to what was going on there that Lovecroft could simply dispose of dead boy "out back"? Therefore, next day, I decided to recruit someone — a young workingman who seemed clean enough — to approach the Asylum gate and ask the bailiff about the boy whose body had been found during the Council visit. He gratefully accepted a shilling and returned an hour later with more news than I had expected.

"Aye," he reported smiling, "they found a boy named Arthur and took his body to the morgue. He'll be buried proper, they say."

"Good," I said.

"There's more too, eh."

"What?"

"It'll cost you another shilling," he said, his hand outstretched. I reluctantly paid. Tucking the coin in his pocket, he continued.

"That day. The day them Council blokes was there, the coppers dragged the Reverend somebody... err... ."

"Lovecroft?"

"Aye, that's the cove. They dragged the bloke out in gyves and led him off to choky, along with some others. A man and fat woman who'd been fairly beaten bloody, they say."

"That would be the Baileys," I explained.

"Didn't catch no names," he said.

As he turned to leave I was tempted to pick his pocket and get back my own, but I'd made a promise to Arthur not to pick the pockets of working folk and I had to stand by it, no matter that he'd robbed me of another shilling.

2

Though Lovecroft had been arrested, I decided not to trust the authorities to do justice by Arthur any more than I trusted the Council — at least not the sort of justice I figured needed to be done. If I guessed right, Lovecroft might be sent to the lockup for stealing money from the County Council, but they'd likely forget all about what was done to Arthur. That's where I decided I would take up the cause. I made an oath to myself that I would see that what was done to my friend was also paid for, in full.

However, that was easier said than done. Lovecroft was out of my reach. I puzzled a day or two about how to do what was needed and for that I decided it would be necessary to reach inside the law. Only a lawyer could do that, and so I set out to find the very best solicitor I could afford.

It wasn't easy to identify just the right person, because I knew nothing of lawyers in London. After some thought, I decided to ask someone who would know such things — someone, who would likely use the services of the best solicitors.

As I sat on a bench on the London Embankment, I noticed that many fine gentlemen and ladies passed, any one of them probably able to tell me what I most wanted to know. I spotted one particularly dapper fellow, with cane and topper, ambling along, apparently enjoying a morning's stroll. I followed and easily picked his side pocket of a very nice coin purse. As he continued down the Embankment, I shouted after him.

"Sir! Sir!"

He turned, surprised, and gave me a guarded look.

"I believe you dropped this," I explained, holding out his purse as I ran up to him.

Still surprised but now smiling, he replied, "Well bless my soul. So I did. Thank you m'lad. I am in your debt," he added, opening the purse and meaning to give me a shilling or two for my service to him.

"That's not necessary, sir," I said, "but there is one thing, if you please."

He frowned and asked, "What then?"

"I would be grateful to you, sir, if you could tell me one thing I need to know."

"What's that?" he asked.

"Could you tell me the name of the best lawyer you know? The best lawyer in London?"

He smiled. "I'm not sure I know that, but I can tell you the man who looks after my affairs. He's certainly one of the best, now you ask me."

"And who is he, please sir?"

"Name's Wallace. Sir Alfred Wallace. You'll find his chambers in the Inner Temple, Number 6, " he added. "You'll also find him quite costly," he said, smiling at the notion I would afford such a solicitor.

"Thank you, kindly, sir," I said, doffing my billycock and turning to leave.

"Good luck, m'lad," he said after me.

"And good luck to you, sir," I said, not bothering to turn.

3

I made my way to the Temple that very afternoon, an area of London, I learned, inhabited by lawyers and centering on the old Temple Church. A bit of inquiry led me to Number 6 — a large old building with a courtyard out front. A plaque on the dooryard gate read Sir Alfred Wallace, Mr. Norman Barfield and Mr. Atherton Smithson. As I looked up at the plaque and considered the impression I would make walking in the door, I braced myself for trouble. As it turned out, I had no idea what a stir I would make.

A short stout man with bulging eyes answered the dooryard bell and looking down seemed to find the very sight of me objectionable and just a little disturbing. I could tell because his eyes opened even wider and his eyebrows shot up about six inches.

I quickly doffed my cap, assumed my most humble facial expression, and bowed deeply, all designed to reassure him I was as harmless as a kitten.

"I would like to see Sir Alfred Wallace, if you please sir," I said, injecting just the right tone of desperation into my voice.

The stout man, who I took to be the porter, snorted once and then uttered a single word — "Preposterous! — before closing the dooryard gate.

That seemed fairly final and all my theatrics had failed miserably. No doubt about that, but I was not to be put off. Reaching into my potato sack for a gold sovereign, I rang the dooryard bell again. And once again the stout porter answered, this time with the look of someone who'd had his fill of urchins.

I said nothing, but held out an open hand, with a gold sovereign shining from the middle of it.

The little man's eyes once more opened wide and his eyebrows shot up. This time, however, snatching up the sovereign he opened the gate and said, "This way, if you please."

I followed him through the chambers door and into a small anteroom filled with several young men who I learned were assistants called clerks, and in front of an ornate door to one side sat a slender woman of middle years, with a long sad face with grey hair done up like a bird's nest of some sort perched on top of it.

The porters said, "A gentleman to see Sir Alfred" and then departed as if his part of the drama was done.

The long woman continued to look at me as if preparing to fend off an attack. I removed my cap once again and said with all the humility I could muster, "If you please, Mum."

All this seemed to put her more at ease, but she stood and advanced on me with an expression on her face that told she intended to pick me up by the scruff of the neck and toss me into the Temple's nearest gutter, making sure that I bounced twice and landed on something sharp. Before she got halfway across the room, I pleaded again.

"Please, Mum, may I have a brief word with Sir Alfred? If you please, Mum."

She stopped and seemed to stagger back just a tad. The very idea that I wanted to see Sir Alfred, rather than rob the chambers' cash drawer, seemed to throw her into indecision.

"See Sir Alfred?" she said in a huff. "See Sir Alfred?" she repeated, this time with a pained expression on her long face, like a hen who'd just laid a hard-boiled egg.

"Yes, Mum. If you please, Mum. 'Tis a matter of great importance, Mum," I continued to plead, wondering if I'd managed just the right combination of humility and despair in my facial expression. The very expression that had not worked very well for me in the recent past.

She rose to her full height, which was considerable, and crossed her arms.

"That's preposterous!" she scoffed. "See Sir Alfred, indeed."

The same word the porter had used, and that put me off.

"It is a matter of great importance, Mum."

"Out with you, boy! Out!" she ordered, her voice both angry and too loud. It brought the inner door open and a small man with reach-me-down side-whiskers and a lush head of white hair stepped out. Somehow, it seemed to me he also had a kindly look in his face, especially about the eyes.

"What on earth's the matter, Mrs. Raeford?" he demanded of the tall woman. He spoke with a Scottish accent.

"This... this boy came in here asking to see you, Sir Alfred. 'Tis a matter of great importance he claims," she said, raising her eyes to the ceiling.

He looked at me and paused for a long moment. Gave me time to make sure the expression on my face looked like I was about to die of something. Finally, he broke the long silence.

"Come in, lad," he invited, standing to one side of his door. I didn't linger with the large, angry woman. I moved right in and found a chair by his desk, my sack of loot resting comfortably on my lap. I heard the woman gurgle as the door close behind me.

Sir Alfred moved to his desk, sat in a large chair, and folded his hands across his stomach.

"What is it then?" he asked, in a slow, compassionate voice. "Why do you wish to see me?"

I considered for the shortest moment and then blurted it out.

"Justice," I said, as if that was enough to satisfy.

He smiled. "I've been at the law for many years, and I tell myself each day that Justice is a fine thing. What sort of Justice do you want?" he asked, still smiling.

"I want justice for my friend, Arthur. That's all I want, sir. I know you are said to be the very best in your profession, so if your profession is Justice, it will mean that I have come to the right man."

I seemed to have put things in a way that Sir Alfred liked, because he leaned forward, his eyes focuses with serious purpose.

"Oh? Well then tell me how I might help Arthur. How I might help him to find Justice, as you put it."

He leaned back in his chair once more, folded his hands across his waistcoat, and waited for me to oblige. I explained all, beginning with my incarceration in St. Cuthbert's, and ending with a description of how Reverend Lovecroft and the Baileys had allow Arthur to die, with no concern at all about him. Sir Alfred listened intently to my story, but his eyes remained stone cold and showed no emotion at all.

When I'd finished he rose from his desk, put his thumbs in the sleeves of his waistcoat, and looked at the window behind him. He stood there a long while and though I was tempted to say more, decided it was best to let him think whatever he was thinking. When he turned back to me, his eyes showed he knew exactly what to do.

"I know very well about Lovecroft, lad. It's been the talk and whisper of legal circles around the Old Bailey for the past week. Though I had no notion of what you tell about your friend Arthur, and 'the others'."

"What do you know, then?" I asked, sensing he was prepared to share it with me.

"Lovecroft was arrested, as you may know, and he was taken into custody and charged. The accusation was embezzlement of Council funds. I understand the proof of his guilt was readily available and apparently he knew it too. That fellow Littlejohn testified against him in return for leniency."

"And what has become of Reverend Lovecroft?" I asked.

"Guilty, of course! The fellow pled guilty, and was sentenced.

"Sentenced to what? Where is he now?"

Sir Alfred frowned. The question seemed to disturb him. He coughed mutely to clear his throat.

"He got a year's incarceration, in Pintonville."

"What! Only a year?" I said.

Sir Alfred looked down at his hands.

"Yes. A lenient sentence, indeed, but the court was inclined to do so in return for a quick plea of guilty and... well... the Council was known to be eager to dispose of the matter and with as little publicity as possible, you can understand."

"Yes, I can," I said, "because they wanted to take no responsibility for allowing Lovecroft and Littlejohn to rob them blind while they were paying no attention."

Sir Alfred's eyes took on a pained expression.

"Yes, boy. I fear you are right, and the court was willing to help conceal their responsibility, for political purposes, I suppose. Not the finest example of Justice, as you call it."

"Doesn't seem to sit well with you, either," I replied quickly, jutting out my chin in a challenging sort of way. I immediately thought my tone would probably make Sir Alfred angry and I would be thrown out. But, instead, he exhaled a sigh and replied, "Yes. You are dead right. It does not sit well with me, especially considering your story of what happened to your friend, Arthur."

Somehow, I was not comforted by Sir Alfred's agreeable attitude. I considered for a long moment what recourse I had.

"You say that Lovecroft is in Pintonville Prison for a year?"

"Aye, and if it is any further consolation to you, the Church has defrocked the good Reverend and he'll likely never find employment again. Well, maybe as a common laborer but that would be the best he could hope."

"Is there any hope of charging Lovecroft with other crimes?" I asked. "There are bodies of boy who died buried out back of the Asylum!"

"I'm afraid not. For one thing, the Council would oppose it. For another, the court would not like to retrace old territory. Things move on in this business... the business of Justice," he added with a sardonic smile. "Evidence would need to be collected and presented to a magistrate, who would have to decide to charge him and place him on remand for trial."

It all seemed final and threw me into another long moment of thinking.

"Would you take on the job of finding evidence that could be presented to a magistrate?" I asked, adding, "I will pay you handsomely for your trouble, win or not."

He gave me a doubtful glance, as if he knew I had no money to pay him. To correct his mistake, I took from my pocket the ten gold sovereigns I'd used to persuade the porter and put them on his desk. His eyes widened and I knew I'd won the point.

"What?" he asked.

"There is a good deal more where that came from. How much would you demand to make the effort?"

The strangeness of my request and the sight of the gold sovereigns seemed at first to rock Sir Alfred a little, if one can be said to rock while seated. He was clearly perplexed, but then, scooping in my ten sovereigns, just as clearly decided it was none of his concern where I'd gotten them.

"As you say, lad. I can make no promises about a charge, but I will gather and present the evidence to the police, and my fee will be 800 pounds."

He said this last with a tone that told me he expected the conversation to end without a bargain. However, I reached into my sack and took out most of the notes and counted 800 pounds out on his desk, as his eyes widened and his mouth fell open an inch or two to the southwest.

"If you can find the Baileys," I advised, "you will likely find a pair who would testify against the Reverend. Mrs. Bailey is his sister, but for a shilling she'd likely tell you where the bodies are buried and then rat all over her dear brothers. She's that sort of person, you understand."

Sir Alfred made a note of the name, while he nodded. "Aye, I'll keep that in mind."

The talk was clearly over and I rose to leave.

"Return in two weeks," he said, opening the door. "I will have something to report by then. In the meantime, do nothing yourself. You'll only get in my way, eh?"

I nodded and said goodbye. The long woman at the desk outside Sir Alfred's door sniffed and gave me a cold glance as I emerged and, I knew, kept a frigid eye on me as I departed, just to ensure that I didn't rob the chambers' cash box on my way out.

CHAPTER NINE
WHEREIN I LIVE BY PICKING LOCKS AND POCKETS

1

After paying Sir Alfred, my sack seemed empty, but I found in it one £5 note. If I ate very little, I reasoned, I might live on it for a few weeks or even a month. But sooner or later, I'd find myself reduced to nothing. I decided to move to one part of London and become very familiar with it because the entire city was just too big to get to know very well in a short time. The neighborhood of the Temple seemed to be a very nice place. So did the district further west — Marylebone, it's called, just south of Regent's Park. But both were too rich for my purse. I decided to venture even further west, toward Paddington Station, north of Hyde Park, and once familiar with it, I made it my new home.

Until now, I had lived mostly on the streets, sleeping in back alley doorways and sometimes in the precincts of a church or public building. Now, I found a room — just off the Edgware Road on the north edge of Paddington — that I could rent by the week for a shilling. It was there that I got my first good sleep in weeks. As I dozed off that night, I thought of Arthur — and how much I missed him and how strange that somehow I seemed fated to be alone in this life.

The next day I spent half a crown to buy myself some better clothes, especially a wool jacket that would protect against the winter cold. Then I began my walks about the neighborhood, becoming familiar with everything that was to be seen. I especially marked the locations of grocers, because I knew that eventually I would be both penniless and hungry and would have to pick a lock or two.

My money ran low before I'd picked any locks, and so my landlady — a kindly woman named Mrs. Haney — said, "You can live in the basement for tuppence a week if you don't mind". I soon learned that what she meant by "don't mind" was if you don't mind the insects — mostly roaches and spiders — and the rodents — mainly rats. I minded, of course, but I figured I could put up with the company for a while until that is I could find work or pick a lock or pocket and afford better. The basement had a door to the outside, up steps, so I found I could come and go without being observed. The door seemed useful too if I had to get out of the house quickly.

The next night, as I prepared for bed, I heard a muffled scratching at the door. A rat in the alley, I figured, but the noise continued, so I rose to investigate. When I opened the door I gasped and fell back a step. It was Cosmo, soaking wet and shivering.

"Bless my soul, laddie; you are slow!" he complained, running into the room. "A guardian angel could freeze out there by the time you responded," he shuddered, while making himself comfortable on my cot. I quickly swiped him to the floor and jumped in myself. As I extinguished my candle and closed my eyes I was quietly horrified that my hallucinations had returned. I decided it was probably because I had eaten very little in the past week.

Then suddenly the candle lighted, as if by itself.

"I know when you're scheming, m'lad. You're plotting to pick locks and pockets and to steal from honest folk, now you've lost all your money... err... I mean to say, all Lovecroft's money."

"Yes. What of it?" I said coldly.

"And what would your dear father, the good vicar, say to that? Aye, you know as well as I. Better to devote yourself to finding work, he'd say."

I did not reply, mainly because I knew he was right. Then I began to wonder why my hallucinations had to be so conscientious and moral. Other fellows in my situation would only think of eating, and damn the sinfulness of it all.

Cosmo went after the rats that very night and made quick work of them. All his effort cost me was a bowl of water every morning.

My search for work proved fruitless. There were no jobs for a boy of my small size and appearance. I found a day's work here and there, but those jobs paid almost nothing. Just enough to keep me in Mrs. Haney's basement, with Cosmo and the roaches. That was good enough as long as I had some money in reserve to buy food, but I soon found myself looking in dustbins in alleys for rotten food discarded from grocers. Most of it was uneatable so I began picking the locks of back doors of grocers to get fresher food. Restaurants too. I found that most of them had cans near the back door where they put stale food to be thrown out when the can was full. It was better food than I was finding in the dustbins — only rotten a few days.

That worked for several nights and I ate pretty well, but then, a grocer caught me. I figured he'd called the copper on the street, but instead, he picked up an old broom handle and gave me a good beating in the alley, one blow landing on my head and drawing blood. I ran faster than the stick and so managed to get away. But now I had blood all over my only coat, which looked a dreadful sight when I tried to find day work. So did the gash in my head and the black eye I had not counted upon.

2

It was then I ran into the gang of toughs who more or less claimed Paddington for their own. They were led by a large boy, with a face like an angry weasel. His name was Georgie, I was told, and pretty soon Georgie and his thugs cornered me in an alley and gave me the lecture about staying out of their way.

"Been watching you, m'lad," said Georgie, dropping the cigarette he'd been smoking, "and don't much like what we've been seein', eh. Time to advise you to stay out of our territory, and that means Paddington," he concluded, gouging my chest with a big, painful finger.

I thought about making some sort of reply but at that moment his face seemed to twist and stretch in a strange way, and his voice became guttural and fierce, like an animal speaking English. It sounded like the taste of horseradish.

"W-e-e kn-o-o-o-w yo-u-u-u-u bee-nnn pickin' l-o-o-ocks, eh," he growled, like some kind of angry dog. Then his eyes turned bright green. That left no doubt in my mind that it was time to run and to my surprise the toughs did not pursue me. I guessed later that they felt they'd delivered their message and frightened me sufficiently to have no more trouble.

The angry weasel's voice told me even more — that I had not left my strange imaginings behind, at St. Cuthbert's. Beyond that, I paid no mind of course, but from then on I had yet another problem—staying out of Georgie's way. Worse, I then heard Cosmo's voice saying again into my mind, "There be demons in this place."

It was easy for me to forget about Lovecroft and all that Sir Alfred was doing for me, because I had more pressing problems — like for example eating and staying out of the way of Georgie and his gaggle of plug-uglies. This last turned out to be easier than I expected at first. I soon learned that Georgie and his thugs mainly stayed around Paddington Station itself, where I supposed they found more people to rob. That left a wide swath of the remaining neighborhood north of the Park for me to feel confident to exploit.

I started picking locks nearer to where I lived and just west of the Edgware Road, toward St. Mary's Hospital. I found that the hospital threw out large quantities of very edible food, so for a time, I didn't have to pick locks. I took my sack each night, cleaned some of the cans out back of the hospital, and returned with enough to enjoy a sort of feast. This held me for several weeks until the hospital's night guard spotted me. He chased me toward home brandishing a great club and cursing all the while. The next night I went later, but he was there again. This happened every time I went back because the foul blighter was on to me and made a regular occupation of anticipating me and chasing me. Soon he started throwing rocks at me as I fled, and when one hit my head and almost knocked me out, I decided to find other sources of garbage, at least for a month or two. Never could figure out why that guard was so keen to prevent me from scavenging his garbage, except that I wasn't allowed to be there and it was his special mission in life to make sure I wasn't. He earned his pay.

3

That created a special problem — where to find food. I managed the next day to find some day labor, and I worked hard, but the job was to move furniture and it was clear to the boss that I just wasn't strong enough to move pieces the way a strong man could. And there were plenty of them around to take my place. Boss was a kind man, and he allowed me to move pieces that were mostly my size, but he was only good for one day. The next day I persuaded a fishmonger to let my help unload wagons of cod that had arrived from Peterhead. It was nasty work, but I kept up with the other workmen. The problem was that the unloading lasted only one day. The good part was that when I got to the basement that night Cosmo had a strange fascination for me and what I'd been doing.

By this means, I lived hand to mouth for a while, but then came a stretch when I couldn't find any work at all, in whatever job. I began to go hungry and once again began to pick locks at the alley doors of restaurants to find fresh garbage. Cosmo and I ate pretty well for a while. I ate the bread, fruit, and vegetables and he got the green fuzzy meat.

I tried to avoid talking to Cosmo, hoping that my imaginings would subside. Soon, however, I could not put aside thinking about the demons — Georgie being just the latest of those hallucinations. I decided Cosmo might have some insights. After all, he had first warned me about the boy Rupert at St. Cuthbert's.

One evening, just as we finished our dinner, I asked, "Cosmo, why do the demons appear to me? What do they want?"

At first he seemed startled by the question or maybe that I was even talking to him. Then he looked puzzled.

"I'm not sure, laddie. I know that demons are prone to be seen, expose themselves you might say, in times of great emotion. They are very emotional. 'Tis one of their weaknesses."

"But, what do they want with me?" I repeated.

"That's something we GAs are not permitted to know, but I can offer an opinion."

"Yes?" I invited.

"Maybe they hate you because you're in their way somehow, or likely to be? Interfering with their schemes, eh?"

What schemes? I wondered.

CHAPTER TEN
WHEREIN I FAIL

1

The next night I was working my way down an alley just off the Edgware Road when I found a door that I thought was the back of a grocery. When I lighted my candle and knelt to have a look at the lock, however, I was startled. Until now, every backdoor lock I had picked was easy. Most were old and cheap and so I had no problem opening them in about a minute. Now, however, I'm sure my mouth dropped open at least an inch to see a lock that even at first glance looked formidable. When I applied my little tools to it, I was even more surprised to find that I was running into internal features I'd never before seen and about which Arthur had never taught me. It was a new thing entirely. It fascinated me and frustrated me at the same time.

As I worked on the thing for about a quarter-hour I learned there were at least three internal mechanisms that were preventing my success, and as I fiddled with them I got an idea of how they worked and also how they looked. After a few more minutes I realized that my tools were not competent to move them and that something new would be required. I was not quite sure what that something new should be, but I could not afford more time to find out. I retreated in defeat for the first time in my lock-picking experience.

2

I don't know which was worse the next day — my empty stomach or the quandary about what would be needed to open that lock. My stomach told me to forget about the lock and find a new grocer. My mind told me that there was nothing more important in this life or the next than opening that bloody lock — even food. Maybe it was the absence of food to disturb my thinking that made things click, but by afternoon I had a good idea of what sort of tool I would need to manipulate the odd parts of the new lock. I began to look around the basement for some things I could fashion into the tool I needed. What I required was a piece of very strong but thin wire, something to help me bend and shape it, and something to help me cut a nick in it and sharpen its end. That was not easy to find, but the basement was full of junk I'd never before taken much interest in and now it gradually yielded everything I needed to make my new tool.

Once I'd found the materials I worked for hours to fashion the tool. Twice I broke the wire and had to start over, but on the third try, I finally figured I'd made the tool I needed.

3

Though I was eager to try my tool on the strange lock, I decided it was more important to return to Sir Alfred's as I had said I would do, mainly to find out how things had gone with my plan for Lovecroft. The strange lock could wait. My taste for getting mine from Lovecroft and ensuring he paid the full price for what he'd done to Arthur was even more important than food. Next day I made my way to the Inner Temple — a considerable walk across London.

The pompous porter let me in, but I knew what awaited me when I entered chambers and I was not disappointed. The long woman swooned a little in her chair and then exhaled a snort that I'm sure rattled windows in the neighboring building. Then she gave me a pained look from her bulging eyes like a snail with a sudden hernia. Still, she said nothing but immediately went to Sir Alfred's study door, knocked, entered and closed it behind her. In a moment she emerged, leaving the door open and stood beside it with her arms crossed and eyes on the ceiling — obviously signaling me to go in. I did not linger.

"Percy, my lad. Come in, please. Come in," Sir Alfred greeted, rising from his desk and gesturing to a chair nearby. "I have just received some news for you." His face seemed troubled.

"About Lovecroft?" I asked, my eyes wide. "He will be charged and brought to trial?"

"It is news about Lovecroft, but not that he will be charged."

"What then?" I asked, a little guarded and preparing for the worst.

"It is a delicate situation, so I must be assured that what I tell you will not leave this room. *Entre quatre murs*, as they say in France."

"Oui. Bien sûr. D'accord," I answered him in French, which seemed somehow to frighten him. When he recovered his composure, he continued.

"Well, I have bad news, I'm ashamed to report."

"Oh?"

"Yes. It is a travesty of justice if even I have seen one. You see, the Lord Chancellor, probably under pressure from the London County Council, has decided to release Lovecroft."

"How's that? How can he do such a thing!" I asked.

"In English justice the Lord Chancellor can do just about anything he bally well wants to do, and in this instance, it is clearly political expediency that has cause the turn of events."

"But, is there anything to be done in reaction? Can the decision be overcome and Lovecroft charged after all?"

"I have done all that's possible at the moment. I filed a protest with the Lord Chancellor, but he quickly rejected it, without cause. There is little that I can do now, but perhaps later."

"Later?"

"Yes. There is a pending Parliamentary election, as you may know. A new government, of the opposing party, may well be more pliable and I may be able to persuade a new Lord Chancellor to reinstate Lovecroft's indictment and put him on trial."

"How much chance of that?" I asked with a frown.

"Very unlikely, but possible. In the meantime, one thing might ease your mind a little."

"Eh?"

"Yes. In most instances where the Lord Chancellor remits sentence and releases an admitted criminal such as Lovecroft, the miscreant is required to leave England and never to return. Lovecroft will go into self-imposed exile and probably without much resource to see him through. With a little luck, he will find a hard life and perhaps his just punishment wherever he decides to go."

I gave it a bit of thought, but then decided it was too little for me.

"That's not good enough, Sir Alfred. Just not good enough. English justice be damned, the blighter Lovecroft should be punished for what he has done — to Arthur and the others!"

"Aye, m'lad. I share your disappointment, but I must say there is nothing to be done at the moment in situation such as this."

He continued to frown in silence for some little while, and so did I. The silence in the room was thick enough to cut with a knife. Then, his face brightened a bit, and he opened a side drawer to his desk.

"There is one other thing I can do that might ease your mind a bit, lad," he said, tossing a purse onto the desk.

"Here is what is left of the retainer you paid me. I feel it is only fair to return what I did not spend. It is a paltry sum, but there it is."

He was right. It did not much satisfy me at first, but I took up the purse and later, when I'd had a chance to consider, it seemed better than nothing in return.

As I left Sir Alfred's chambers and the Temple, I carried with me a sense of defeat. But as I walked, I decided that although I was blocked for the moment, Lovecroft was out there somewhere, enjoying a freedom he did not deserve, and I would make it my future business to see him back in prison and perhaps on the scaffold.

CHAPTER ELEVEN
WHEREIN I AM CAUGHT!

1

My sense of failure concerning Lovecroft almost made me give up everything in despair. It was Cosmo who shook me out of my melancholy. Well, Cosmo and hunger.

"Laddie, you must see this as only a momentary setback. Look at you. You are young and talented and you have a whacking good head on your shoulders to top it all. You'll find a way. All that's needed is to trust in your future."

Cosmo's view of the thing seemed reasonable to me. There was yet time to achieve something and after all Lovecroft was out there somewhere. He could not evade being found eventually and maybe he did not even bother about hiding. So far, he had evaded justice and why shouldn't he think that he could do so forever. I would find a way to see him punished for what he'd done to Arthur and the others.

Meanwhile, there was the need to eat. The money that Sir Alfred had returned to me amounted to a pittance of what I'd paid. It was enough to see us through a hard stretch, but I decided to put most aside as savings and to make my way by my lock picking trade. The best part was that it provided a bit of food to see me through.

Still, there was that lock I had found so interesting to be overcome and now I devoted myself to that task. I had made my tool and so I was ready to go out and make another try. The food didn't matter a wit right now. I was determined to get the best of that lock.

It began to rain almost the minute I left the basement next evening, and as I reached my objective I was soaked to the marrow. Still, I was determined and nothing could persuade me not to try my new tool on that bloody lock. My candle of course would not be lighted in the rain, so I stood for a long while in an alley doorway, hoping the rain would stop long enough for me to try my luck. It didn't.

I crouched in the doorway for nearly an hour, as the storm gave no sign of relenting. I began to think about returning to the basement and trying again the next night when suddenly the rain stopped.

I doubted I'd seen the last of the rain, but I dashed to the lock bending over my lighted candle to protect it from the rain. That didn't work. I needed both hands to work on the lock and so I had to make do with the dim light that filtered into the alley from a nearby street lamp. I worked quickly with my new tool and at first, it seemed too large and bulky to reach into the lock and do what I wanted it to do, but a few minutes learning to use it gave better results. I moved one mechanism easily, and then another, and on the third, had some trouble, but eventually managed to push it aside too. After that, the lock acted like a regular lock and I opened it in a matter of a minute or two.

When the mechanism clicked and I knew the door was open, I felt a rush of achievement. Still, I waited a moment to push open the door, but when I did, I found an even greater surprise than the unusual lock. There was no kitchen and no can filled with fresh garbage. By the glow of my relighted candle, I could not at first tell what sort of room I was in, but a bit of stumbling around and looking here and there told me I was in a workshop of sorts — a workshop with all kinds of tools hanging on the walls, above a long workbench. There were stools, a big table, with odd tools on it, and a closed-door leading who knew where. But no can with fresh garbage.

"What is this place?" I wondered. *"Not a kitchen, for sure."*

After a moment's quandary, I was surprised and intrigued by the look of the room, but then my heart sank to think that I'd done all that work and still my stomach would be empty for another day. I turned to leave and just as my hand touched the door, a low, deep voice from behind me said, "Put up your hands — slowly."

Then the light came up. I'd been caught once again. Last time I'd been beaten with a broomstick and I expected the same in about five seconds. However, there was nothing but an eerie silence, as whoever had given me the order remained still and said no more. Then he said, "Turn slowly, with your hands in the air."

2

I did as told, and when I turned I saw an old man in his dressing gown and nightcap, holding a lantern in one hand and a whacking big pistol in the other. He looked like the sort who'd shoot about anyone who made him angry, so I smiled. It was a hollow, mirthless smile, but I figured it would be the best thing I could do in the circumstances. Friendly, you know. It did no good with the old man. He continued to frown and worse, he continued to point the ugly pistol at my nose.

Then I noticed peering out from behind the old man there stood a ginger-haired girl in a bathrobe. She had freckles and two big eyes with an evil look in both of them.

"He looks to be a dangerous blackguard, Grandpapa. Notice the bushy hair. That criminal face. He's a killer if ever I saw one. Better shoot him now," said the squirt. The girl's attitude seemed to me to lower the tone of what was already a very testy situation. I gave her a withering look and she wilted a little and moved behind the old man. Happily the old buster was having none of her hurtful suggestion about shooting me.

"Shush, Hannah. I'll tend to this," he said. "Who are you?" he demanded, now waggling his pistol right in my face. He had a long sallow face, with big sad eyes and a long thin nose. He also had a long thin beard and stringy hair, both white. Meanwhile, the girl continued to goggle at me from behind the old man.

"Percy," I said. "Percy St.-John."

"What are you doing in here?"

I gulped. "Looking for garbage. I thought this was a grocery."

"For garbage? What for?"

"To eat. I'm hungry."

His face softened a little, but the squirt was having none of it. "A big lie if ever I heard one," she scoffed. "You better shoot him now, before he strangles both of us and throws our bodies in the river. They'll find our bloated corpses floating in the Thames."

"How'd you get in here?" the old man asked, again ignoring the girl's suggestion.

"I picked the lock."

"You picked that lock?" he said, eyes wide and nodding toward the door.

"Yes. That one."

"How'd ye do that?"

I swallowed hard.

"It's what I do. I'm a picklock," I said, jutting out my chin. "It was a tough one, however. Never saw a lock like that one."

The old man smiled faintly.

"Yes. It was made to be hard to pick."

"It was. The first night I tried it, I failed. Had to go home and make a special tool to get the job done, but tonight I succeeded."

"A tool. Let me see that tool."

I lowered one hand, reached into my jacket pocket.

"Look out, Grandpapa! He's going for a knife for sure," said the befreckled little pestilence. "Better shoot the bounder and be done with it."

I slowly pulled out the special tool I'd made and held it up to the lamp. The old man looked at it with great interest. At first, he frowned, but then he smiled. I noticed that the girl had stepped out into the room and was still frowning.

"That is quite good," he exclaimed, lowering his pistol. "You can lower your hands, but put that tool on the workbench, there," he nodded.

"What!" the squirt shouted. "He'll murder us for sure, Grandpapa!"

3

I did as he said, and then there was a long silence, as he looked me over. I sized him up too. Finally, I spoke.

"You're a Jew, aren't you?"

"How do you know?" he snapped.

"Your nose and color."

He frowned and snorted.

"Have you ever heard the word 'Semitic'," he asked

"No."

"It's where the nose comes from. It's a facial feature that's shared by a large population of people who live in the Eastern Mediterranean world and not just Jews. Many Muslims and Christians too, eh. But you are right; I am a Jew."

"Oh."

"You don't much like Jews, eh?"

I looked at the pistol to see where he was pointing it.

"No, I don't."

"You see, Grandpapa," the girl exclaimed. "He's a Jew-hater. Murders Jews by the scores, I'll wager."

"Why?" the old man asked me. "Why don't you like Jews?"

"Can't trust a Jew about money. That's why," I explained, thinking he'd point the pistol at me again. He did, and then he harrumphed once and then snorted again, only louder. It was probably the loudest snort I'd ever heard. Even louder than the long, snail-eyed woman at Sir Alfred's chambers. It was the kind of epic snort that in later years you'll devote three pages to describing in your memoirs.

"You see Grandpapa," the girl screeched; "he's a Jew-hating criminal lunatic. Shoot that son-of-a-bachelor and be done with it. That's what I say."

"You *can* trust a gentile to be bigoted, ignorant, and pigheaded, and especially a gentile boy who breaks into a Jew's shop in the middle of the night to rob him," the old man replied. "What d'ye say your name was, boy?" the old man asked.

Meanwhile, the malevolent little pill seemed to have an overwhelming hostility toward me and gave me the evil eye throughout.

"Percy. Percy St.-John. My mother named me Percival," I said. "And I wasn't going to rob anybody. I told you, I thought this was a grocery." I frowned toward the girl and gave her a crinkled nose.

"The grocer's next door. You opened the wrong back door."

You can say that again, I was thinking, as the old man pulled up a stool and sat.

"And I'm not ignorant. I can read."

Now the girl snorted. She was clearly well on the way to developing a snort that would equal her Grandpapa's in only a few more years.

"Read, eh?"

"Yes. I can even read that sign on the wall."

He looked at the sign then turned to me, puzzled.

ומתוקנים נעזרים מנעולים

"It says 'LOCKS MADE AND REPAIRED'."

"What? You can read Hebrew! How on earth...."

"My father taught me. He also taught me to read and speak Latin and French. He was a vicar and he learned languages at Cambridge."

His mouth fell open and remained that way for the next minute or so, as he scratched his chin whiskers and looked from me to the sign and back several times. The girl's scowl seemed to fade a bit too.

"Where is your father now?"

"Dead. He was murdered."

He released a sigh, and then said, "Sit," nodding toward a nearby chair and still pointing his pistol at me. Then he picked up the tool and began to examine it closely, but kept an eye on me all the while.

"This is quite good," he said, holding the tool up to his eyes. "How did you think of it?"

"Well, I worked on the lock the night before and I couldn't open it, but I got a good idea what the insides looked like. Then I imagined what sort of tool would be needed to move those odd parts. And that's when I knew how to make my tool."

He smiled. "That is very good. You impress me with your knowledge of locks."

I said nothing, figuring the angry old man sounded like he might decide to let me go. Then he surprised me.

"Well, Percival, how would you like to come work for me? As my shop boy? You have broken into a locksmith's shop, as you now know, where I also sell strong boxes and safes."

"But Grandpapa," the girl exclaimed.

I gave the offer about a half-second's careful consideration, and then answered.

"Sure! I'd like that. I can use the work."

He smiled and nodded. "You'll start tomorrow morning at 7. That's when I open my shop. My name is Finermann — Tobias Finermann. This is my granddaughter, Hannah. You'll see the name on the front of the shop when you come back to work. Use the front door this time," he said, with an ironical tone in his voice.

With that, I left quickly by the back door, not wanting to linger in case he changed his mind and decided to hail the local copper after all. When I reached home I explained the situation to Cosmo, and he agreed with me that our food situation now looked much better than it had a day or two ago, though he always seemed to have a ready supply of basement rats.

I wondered why a guardian angel would be eating mice and rats, but I never asked Cosmo. I figured he had a cat nature that made him do such things, despite his better — angelic — self. Then I reminded myself that any insane thing Cosmo was doing was just a further elaboration of my own mental illness.

CHAPTER TWELVE
WHEREIN I BECOME A SHOP BOY

1

The next morning, as I made my way down the Edgware Road toward Mr. Finermann's shop, I smiled at my good fortune in finding work that would teach me even more about locks, tough I still cringed a bit at the attitude of the small, red-headed monster living in the shop. If Mr. Finermann's other locks were anything like the one on the back door, I figured I was in for a real treat. And, to think I'd be paid for my work.

As I reached the shop and tried the front door, it was still locked. So, I took time to examine the lock. It was different from the back, and as I knelt to get a closer look, I heard a stern voice from behind me.

"Hoy! What's this m'lad? Thinkin' 'bout breakin' that lock, are ye?"

I turned with a start, only to see a policeman—frowning, holding a long baton, and pointing it at me. I raised my hands without being told.

"I... I am... I am examining this lock," I explained.

"Aye, I can see that. Preparin' to pick it, I'd guess, eh?"

Just then the door opened and Mr. Finermann stepped out.

"Caught this lad preparin' a felonious assault upon your lock, Mr. Finermann," said the copper, now rocking on his big feet and beating the baton in his left hand.

"Thank you, officer Medley, but this boy is my new shop boy. His name is Percival and this is his first day at the job."

I smiled and stood. Officer Medley said, "Ho," which I took to be his favorite word, and then moved on. We watched him amble down the Edgware Road.

"Come in, boy. Come in," Mr. Finermann invited. "You'll start by watching me fashion the parts for a new lock I am making, not unlike the one on the front door. Some slight design difference, because I am forever trying to improve my works."

Just then the squirt appeared from somewhere, this time dressed in a smock dress and carrying a leather satchel on her shoulder. And with her, a small woman of middle years with a jolly face.

"Off to school, my dear," Mr. Finermann encouraged. "Mustn't be late, eh," he smiled.

She gave me the evil eye again, but said nothing as she disappeared out the front door.

"Hannah goes to the girl's school just up the road. She's a fine student," he said smiling proudly after her. "Oh yes," he continued, "this fine woman is Mrs. Wambly. She arrived just before you and let herself in with her key. Mrs. Wambly cooks and cleans for Hannah and me and generally takes good care of us. I might add that she is the best in her trade.

The small woman laughed heartily and then proceeded upstairs and to her duties.

I took a stool at his workbench and observed closely as he used his tools to file and cut and shape pieces for his locks. I also watched closely as he used several hand and treadle-driven machines to grind down, cut, and fashion pieces of metal for the lock. It was amazing to me that there were such machines and that Mr. Finermann used them all with such skill and quiet precision. Watching him, I wanted to do it myself, and as expertly as he did it.

After what seemed like only a few minutes, he looked up at me and said, "Time for our midday meal. Have you brought something?"

"Err... ah... no. I have not had a midday meal in quite some time," I said.

"Well, you shall today. Mrs. Wambly will share her special bean soup with you. A receipt she has from her dear mamma, who was a fine cook, especially around a bean. A good midday meal is included in your pay. Just as is your room to sleep."

I was stunned that room and board came with the job. I smiled broadly and could hardly help but let out a cheer.

Mrs. Wambly's soup was every bit the delicious mixture Mr. Finermann had said, and after we had finished our soup and black bread, he took me to a small room just off the workshop. It was a storage room of sorts, but with a cot and small chair.

"This room was occupied by my previous shop boy. His name was Nick and he has since moved on to Devon, where he has set up in his own shop. He's a good lad and will make a success of himself, I believe."

I was grateful for the place to sleep, and right at my new work, but I hesitated to tell Mr. Finermann about Cosmo. Not about him being a guardian angel, of course, but about him being an ugly cat and a good mouser. Finally, I decided that I could not avoid the subject, so I confessed that I had a cat friend who must come with us to live in the shop. Mr. Finermann thought for a moment and then said, "You know, I'd never considered the need for a shop cat, but now you mention it, we do have a supply of mice running about the place and instead of trapping, perhaps it would be more efficient to employ an expert. Bring Cosmo with you and welcome to him as well."

2

Next morning, with Cosmo safely stored in my sack, I moved into our new room, and while I continued my lessons in making lock parts with Mr. Finermann, Cosmo went to work on the local mouse population. It wasn't long before Mr. Finermann exclaimed, "Look! He's found one!" as Cosmo dashed across the shop after an elusive mouse. He smiled. "Earning his keep already."

In the next weeks, I learned more each day from our *lessons* at the workbench and Mr. Finermann said I was a "quick study". Soon, I too was making parts on my own; under his direction and close instruction and a while later, I was fashioning whole locks. In only a short while, I was schooled enough in the locksmith trade that Mr. Finermann said I was capable of doing my own work, and he needed not to watch me so closely. That increased substantially the amount of work the shop could do and Mr. Finermann declared, "You are both worth your keep, finally, like Cosmo". He increased our wages a little, saying that "because of you, Percival, the shop is now into even more profit".

During this time, also, Hannah grew accustomed to my presence and appeared to reconcile in her own mind that I was not a criminal after all and that, to her surprise, I was a good worker and useful to the shop. In these new circumstances, she began to loaf around the shop when she returned from school, but she had no role in the work. Mr. Finermann insisted that she must do her home study, which in her case seemed to be reading.

Hannah referred to Mrs. Wambly as "Auntie," probably because the happy little woman had taken care of her since she was a small child and had become a sort of substitute mother to her. I never heard talk of Hannah's mother and father, so I supposed that it was a painful episode in the Finermann family story. Hannah meanwhile helped with the cleaning in the shop and seemed delighted to be around Mrs. Wambly.

As I also learned later, Hannah's reading consisted almost entirely of the new detective fiction in *The Strand Magazine*, mostly stories associated with that popular fellow, Sherlock Holmes. I didn't care for that sort of reading myself, but Hannah couldn't get enough of it and even seemed to filter everything in her life's reality through the lens of such stories. Needless to say, she had a fairly warped view of humanity, especially for a young pill.

It wasn't easy to chat with Hannah, but one day she seemed to need to tell me something, so I listened attentively.

"I'm a palindrome," she said with her chin raised high and standing up to her full height, which wasn't much.

I had noticed that, but I decided to say, "Oh?"

"Yes. Not everyone has a name that's spelled the same backwards and forwards."

"Oh, that is quite different. Yes, very few people I should think."

"You, for example, are an *y-crep*, which sounds like the mangled corpse of something Cosmo would bring in from the alley."

It was the sort of remark that deserved a whack about the ears, but I decided to let it go. On closer thought I decided I was fortunate she did not begin calling me *ee-crep*.

Hannah was studying French at school and when she learned I could speak it fluently she insisted that we should speak it to each other at the shop. This was fine with me, but unfortunately Mr. Finermann and Mrs. Wambly could not follow what we were talking about.

Her enthusiasm for speaking French encouraged Hannah to open up and tell me all about her plans and aspirations.

"I am going be a great artist," she proclaimed one day. "When I've finished at my private school I intend to go to the Slade School and study art with the best. Then to Paris and the Ecole des Beaux-Arts."

"That's a fine plan," I agreed, "but difficult. You'll be challenged."

"I can do it," she sniffed, as if I doubted her. "I am a very good artist, and I will be even better. Only... ." she stopped herself to consider.

"Eh?" I encouraged.

"Only, I might decide to be a detective. Grandpapa says I have a great talent for such things and I believe he is quite right."

"Oh?"

"Yes. Suppose you enter the library of Sir Geoffrey Sinclair and he is lying face down on the carpet, in a pool of his own blood, with a dagger of Chinese design in his back. What would you make of it?" She asked, giving me a sidelong look, her eyes narrowed.

"Well, I'm not sure I would ──."

"You'd know," she stopped me, "that poor Sir Geoffrey was killed by a Chinese murderer who might me working for the Tong." She gave me a look that said I should be mighty surprised at her detecting talents.

"Maybe it means that Sir Geoffrey was a collector of oriental artifacts and whoever killed him snatched up a knife from his desk, which he used to open envelopes, and put it right between his second and third thoracic vertebrae," I said. "Personally, I suspect strongly that he was murdered by his secretary, Mr. Oswald Poole, who wanted to marry Sir Geoffrey's daughter, Marvis, but who Sir Geoffrey rejected as unsuitable."

She sniffed and returned to her reading.

Hannah's obsession with the new mystery thriller novels went far to explain her view of life, and especially me. She confided to me with some hesitation that she knew I was a criminal lunatic, even if her Grandpapa believed otherwise, and she was on her guard constantly, knowing that sooner or later I would loot the shop and lock both of them in the storeroom to cover my escape.

I noticed that after school — when not reading about detective derring-do — Hannah spent long hours with pad and pencil in hand, sketching things around the shop, including me. She seemed particularly fascinated by Cosmo and of course he willingly posed for endless drawings. I suspect he was the most sketched guardian angel in the history of mankind.

Mr. Finermann was an observant Jew, and always wore his little cap — the *yamaka*. He also kept the Shabbat — or Sabbath, as my father would have said. Only in Mr. Finermann's case, the Shabbat began on Friday evening and lasted until Sunday. That meant we closed early on Fridays—at 3 o'clock and did not reopen until Monday mornings. Hannah accompanied him to synagogue and so during that time, Cosmo and I were on our own. I spent much of that time walking about Paddington and nearby parts of London — south well into Hyde Park — and learning all about the city. I came to enjoy and to love it quite as much as any native-born Londoner because there was something about London that appealed to the deep Englishness in me. I had not expected that at first, because I was lonely for my village. During this time there was no need to practice my lock picking or pocket-picking trades. Cosmo, like me, was well provided with food and I even had a bit of ready money to spend. Most of my wages however went into a can that I kept under my cot, against the day that I might once again find myself on the streets and hungry.

As I worked I noticed that Hannah began to observe me almost as much as she watched Cosmo. I supposed she was curious that I had not yet murdered her Grandpapa with a meat cleaver. Having studiously avoided speaking to me for a week, she suddenly decided that I needed to be interrogated, in French of course.

"How old are you?" she asked unexpectedly one afternoon, as she hovered over my workbench.

"Ten," I said. "How old are you?"

"I'm not sure you need to know," she replied, jutting out a belligerent chin, "but since you asked, I'm eleven." She seemed terribly proud to be older than me. Then she lapsed into silence, spending her time making a sketch of me at the workbench. She carefully avoided showing it to me, I suppose because she added horns to my head. Thereafter, however, she seemed to take a more relaxed attitude toward me and even made friendly comments.

3

One evening when Cosmo and I were alone in the sleeping room, we fell into another conversation about guardian angels. I'm not sure how the subject arose, but I asked him if he could see other guardian angels, roaming about the place.

"Oh yes," he said. "Hannah's guardian angel, for example, is always about. He's a big, handsome brute with nicely oiled blond hair, a flowing robe of shimmering white silk and of course, a pair of wings that must be at least 20 feet across. Quite a sight to see."

"He must be one of the successful guardian angels," I observed, daring to raise a sensitive subject with Cosmo.

"Oh yes. He has a reputation for being among the best. Hannah is lucky to have him and I'm sure he will do her a bit of good over the years."

Considering Hannah's personality I was having a bit of trouble seeing her guardian angel as "successful," but I let it go.

"How about the others?" I led on.

"Oh, I have seen Mr. Finermann's guardian angel, but he's rather a furtive sort and not one to linger about."

"And Mrs. Wambly?"

"Can't say I've ever seen him yet, but then some GAs keep to themselves and don't flit about."

"Could that mean that Mrs. Wambly is not well? Or, not as well as she seems," I asked.

"I don't know," said Cosmo, shrugging his shoulders. "Perhaps. I don't know what it means. Or, that it means anything.

I hesitated to raise the subject, but my curiosity got the better of me.

"Are... err... are ———."

"Let's have it, lad," he encouraged.

"Are any guardian angels like you? I mean, having the form of a cat or other creatures?"

He hesitated, but did not seem angry.

"Aye. I once knew a fellow GA named Horace, who was a donkey."

"A donkey!" I repeated, surprised. "How do you suppose he got to be that way?"

"Made a damned ass of himself, I guess!" he said and then broke into riotous laughter that sent him rolling about the floor.

CHAPTER THIRTEEN
WHEREIN I FIND SUCCESS AND DESPAIR

1

Mr. Finermann's shop specialized in fine locks, from which its profits mainly came. Most of our work was devoted to making and repairing locks. However, while I worked at locks, Mr. Finermann sometimes went to another room in the shop, where he also repaired and remade safes and strong boxes. This sideline business did not interest me at first, because I saw myself then as a locksmith and I assumed my life's work would concern locks. I wanted the learn all I could about them.

One day, however, Mr. Finermann invited me to join him in repairing a particular kind of safe and his introduction to this work changed my life. From that morning, as he led me into the delicate mechanisms that created the combinations governing the locks of safes, I knew at once that I'd found something more intricate than mere door locks and that fascinated me. By the end of that day, I knew my craft would be safes and vaults.

For the next several weeks — in part because Mr. Finermann's safe work had picked up — we divided our time between locks and safes. At that time Mr. Finermann had six safes of various manufacture and age in the shop for repair and so I got a broad education in the subject. One day, however, with a playful tone in his voice, Mr. Finermann asked me if I would like to know the greatest fun with safes.

"Of course," I replied, not quite knowing what he had in mind.

"Lock that safe," he instructed, turning his head away.

I did as he told me.

"I have the combination of that safe on the repair order, but I do not know it."

I nodded because I knew that was the usual thing.

"Now observe closely," he said, still with a subtle smile in his eyes.

I leaned in, while he began to listen to the mechanism as he worked the safe's knob. Then, reaching into a drawer, he took out a doctor's horn—the sort of device that a physician would use to listen to your heart or that a deaf person would use the help them hear. He held the horn to the safe's door and worked at the combination lock. He turned it this way and that, noting as he went something that I could not know. After he had done this for so long that I figured he was completely lost, he stood back, looked at the nob, wrote something on a paper, and then in his very direct way, worked the combination. When he'd finished, he instructed me, "Alright, Percival. Open the safe."

I took hold of the latch handle, pulled it down, and then drew the door. I am sure my mouth fell open at least as wide as the door opened. Still agog, I looked first at the open safe and then at Mr. Finermann, who stood by smiling proudly.

Although I saw him work the safe's lock, I still did not know how he had done it.

"How'd you do that?" I gasped.

"That's what you will learn in the next month or so. That, and much more.

2

He was right. As we worked at both safes and locks over the next month, I could see from the expressions on his face and the sound of his voice that Mr. Finermann held a special regard for safes. Maybe he infected me with those feelings, because I soon felt the same fascination and the same preference. By the end of our first week's work on safes, I knew I was a safe man.

It was now spring and everything seemed to be going quite well for Cosmo and me also. Mr. Finermann developed a true fondness for Cosmo and for me too it seemed to me. He paid me regularly and while I had to buy a bit of food for myself at the grocer next door, I was able to save most of what I made. And, with so many safes and strong boxes to choose from, I had no problem storing my savings safely. With proper food and a warm place to live I could not think of more to ask.

Mr. Finermann was generous with my pay, especially considering that I probably made very little profit for him in my first months. With my savings, I decided to take advantage of the opportunity to buy a velocipede from the grocer next door. It was in pretty bad shape, but with Mr. Finermann's mechanical help and a little expense I put it in good working order in only a few days. Hannah enjoyed it as much as I, and Mr. Finermann laughed heartily to see her ride it.

Hannah had a generous weekly allowance from Mr. Finermann and so asked me if she could buy a half share of the bicycle. I agreed.

I saw the bicycle as a good way to get around the Paddington neighborhood, but Hannah soon had the ambition to join a touring club of other female enthusiasts. We both road the bicycle as much as possible and often together, with Hannah on the handlebars. She screeched gleefully as we flew up and down the streets of Paddington.

One day in mid-May, as we worked on a particularly difficult American-made safe, Mr. Finermann suddenly looked at me with an odd gleam in his eye, and said, "Percival, it is now time for you to learn the fine points of opening safes. I hesitate to teach you because I know you have been a picklock and a thief, and so I must have your promise that you will only use what I teach you for good, and not for evil purposes. Many learn this trade who use it for evil, just as do the picklocks."

I quickly agreed with what he proposed. "Yes, I promise to use my skills for good and not for evil," I said, raising my chin a little belligerently as I said it, as if a bit peeved to be challenged in that way.

"Good. Now, we can begin some earnest work. It will complete your education as a safe man, and I will be proud of you."

By this time I had developed such respect and fondness for Mr. Finermann that he gave me a good feeling to think he would be proud of me. I already felt that from our work together, but to hear him say it was wonderful. I was also ashamed of my old attitude toward Jews and I told him so. He smiled and gave me a gentle knock on the top of my head.

"I won't disappoint you, Mr. Finermann," I pledged, and he commenced immediately to teach me how to open safes, cold. I sensed it was now time for me to become the expert I wanted to be.

"This is a particularly good safe to begin because it is both a common sort of lock and yet has modern features that are confusing. The Americans are devilishly clever about safes, so be careful of their work," he warned. "American safes are almost always complicated in some way."

That moment began my education in the tricky art of opening safes. Mr. Finermann explained that someone who required a safe to be opened without destroying its locking mechanism often called him out. This required the special skills of a cracksman. This was the first time I heard the word "cracksman," which is what I ultimately became.

I recalled that he had sometimes been called out and took with him a sack of his tools, but I had only thought that someone required a lock to be replaced or repaired. I'd never considered that he might be going out to open a safe.

Except for the period of Shabbat, I never knew Mr. Finermann to go out at night or to return to the shop at night. His rooms were above the shop and so I could usually hear him when he and Hannah returned on Friday evenings and other evenings from synagogue. Mrs. Wambly usually completed her duties and left about 6 o'clock, and sometimes Mr. Finermann worried that she was walking home alone in the dark of evening.

One night, some months after I had first started in the shop, I suddenly awakened in the middle of the night. At first, I had no idea why. I had heard no noise. Cosmo was quiet. As I lay there, however, thinking that I would be quick to return to sleep, the whole of my sleeping room began to glow and then filled with a faint blue and pulsating light. At first, I thought I was having a nightmare, but quickly confirmed to myself I was awake. Next, I decided it must be Cosmo doing something, but he was nowhere about. Then I heard it. A voice, which was at first so faint I could not make out what it was saying. But then, the blue glow grew brighter and the voice came loud enough for me to hear its whisper. It was saying, "Beware. There be demons in this place." It repeated the warning several times, always in a whisper and each time striking greater terror in my spirit.

When I finally understood the voice, it and the blue glow disappeared, and all was dark and quiet and strangely I was no longer terrified either. In fact, as I lay in my cot for an hour thinking about what I had seen and heard, I realized that it had not left me frightened at all and somehow that was the oddest thing about it. Then I wondered; had it been merely another of my wild imaginings — an hallucination? Or, was it real and therefore something I should take seriously? I had not recognized the voice and I was sure it was not Cosmo. As I considered such things, I drifted back to a dreamless sleep.

In the next days I thought often about the strange, whispered message, so much like what Cosmo had told me at St. Cuthbert's. I decided that whatever it was — probably one of my crazy imaginings — it did not seem to be harmful and I was still a little surprised that I was not alarmed by it. In the coming days I had more serious things to think about, so the whisper disappeared from my thoughts.

3

Questions about Mr. Finermann's doings soon took a distant place in my mind. In the next week I decided it was not too early to revisit Sir Alfred to see if he had found any prospect of returning Lovecroft to prison. As I approached the dooryard gate I drew up my trousers, set my jaw and prepared for whatever the long woman delivered. The porter showed me in and seeing me, the woman's face assumed a look like something didn't smell quite right. Sir Alfred was welcoming, but at the same time his eyes betrayed bad news.

"Have a seat young Percy," he invited. Once seated he folded his hands over his stomach, erred-and-ahed a bit, and then told his story.

"I've had a bit of a shock just this morning, and I fear it will distress you as well. Might as well get it out, however."

"What?"

"Lovecroft has disappeared and his whereabouts are entirely unknown. Even the Government does not know where he has gone and cannot say that he has gone abroad, as they usually require."

"But... ." I stammered, ". . . but how could that be? How can he have just disappeared?"

"I am not yet sure what happened, but it seems to me that he would have required an extraordinary assistance of some kind to escape the detection of the authorities. Causes me to scratch my increasingly hairless head, for sure."

"But is there nothing to be done?"

"I fear not, m'lad. I have little doubt that the Council will press the authorities to drop the matter. You see, it's those troublesome bodies 'buried out back.' The Council would just as soon forget about something like that, which happened on their watch. Much as they might like to punish Lovecroft, they are far more concerned to protect their own reputations. A scandal of the sort that Lovecroft's testimony or confession would unleash would almost certainly destroy the political careers of every man on the Council."

"So the death of Arthur and the others is to be swept under the carpet, to protect the Councilmen themselves, never mind that Lovecroft may be living the good life in England?"

Sir Alfred closed his eyes and leaned back in his chair.

"Yes. I fear so," he finally said in a low voice.

I sensed there was no more to be said. My effort to get justice for Arthur had come to a dead end. Though Sir Alfred offered to keep me informed of all he should find out in the future, I left his chambers knowing that I had been defeated. I could think of no further way to search for Lovecroft and see that he was held accountable. My next emotion was that I had failed Arthur and "the others" who Lovecroft had allowed to die. For the longest time I could not help seeing Arthur's frail and sad face, peering at me in his disappointment.

CHAPTER FOURTEEN
WHEREIN HANNAH FINDS A DEMON

1

By next morning my feelings had turned from defeat to resolve. I would find some way to bring Lovecroft to justice for his crimes, no matter what. But that effort would need to wait, because my immediate problem was to make good in my new line of work. I worked harder than ever at my bench and Mr. Finermann smiled his satisfaction with my efforts.

In the meantime, I found that Hannah became much more chatty, apparently having decided that I would probably not strangle her and Mr. Finermann in their sleep. One of the things she wanted especially to convey to me was the strange goings-on that had stirred quite a sensation at her school in the past week. I was not interested in her story at first, but I told myself it was important to humor her if I wanted to keep my situation with Mr. Finermann.

She came to my small room one evening, just as Cosmo and I finished the soup and black bread that Mrs. Wambly had brought us. Well, actually Cosmo was finishing something indescribable that he had found in the ally an hour earlier, which I assumed had been a living creature at one time. Usually, Hannah just walked in on us, but this time she knocked and said my name. I said, "Come in."

Frowning, her mouth pursed, and her eyes downcast, it was clear from first glance that something was amiss. I feared that something might be wrong with Mr. Finermann.

"What is it?" I said, as she took a seat on the stool beside my cot. I noticed that Cosmo had let go his dinner and was also alert to hear what came next.

"Percy, I must tell you something. If I don't tell someone I'll pop and I dare not tell Grandpapa because it might distress him. I just have to tell someone," she repeated, chewing an anxious lower lip.

I was a little puzzled why she had chosen me as the someone to tell, but I was still eager to please.

"Oh? What's that?"

"It's about school. You know. My private school. Mrs. Amberson's Academy for Girls. Near the Hospital."

Except for passing it a few times, the school had not made much impression on me, but I gave it a knowing "Ah yes."

"Something's been going on the past week or so and it has some of us girls worried." Her eyes opened wide, with just a touch of anxiety in them. "Frightened even."

It wasn't like Hannah to be frightened. Off the deep end, sure, but not frightened. "Something like what?" I followed, now more interested.

"Not just one thing, but several. All strange and unnerving. Even my friend Elsie says they are odd, and she's not one to be going off without a reason. Elsie says it all bears watching."

"I still don't know what you're talking about, but I'll take your word that Elsie is as stable as the British Empire. What are you and Elsie watching?"

Sitting bolt upright, she now relaxed noticeably and began her narrative.

"It started about a week ago, as I said, in one of the school's lavatories. One of the lower form girls, named Maggie, was using the room. In it there's a closet for storing towels and such, right?"

"Yes. Go on."

"Maggie swears she heard a muffled noise coming from the closet — a sound she took to be a mouse."

Cosmo perked-up.

"Was it?"

"No. She says when she opened the door there stood in the closet an old man dressed all in black. A tall, thin man with long side-whiskers and a tall hat. She says he had a scowl on his face that would frighten a saint."

"What did she do?"

"She slammed the closet door and ran from the lavatory, screaming like a soul in torment. The classrooms emptied out to see what the matter was, of course, but Maggie was so upset she could only howl for several minutes. When she was finally able to tell her story to Miss Drummond — one of the schoolmistresses — we all listened with our mouths hanging open about six inches or more. I thought mine was going to fall off its hinge. Miss Drummond ventured carefully down to the lavatory — thinking she would find a man in there who'd wandered in off the street — but when she opened the closet there was nothing but towels and washcloths. No scowling old man in black."

The Headmistress sent Maggie home on sick report, until she felt just right. That took a day or two.

"You said there were *things* — other strange happenings, eh?"

"I'll say there were! Maggie's fright was only the first."

I was now fully absorbed in Hannah's story, and eagerly waiting for her to tell the rest. Unfortunately, she lapsed in to silence for a long moment, while Cosmo and I exchanged puzzled glances.

"Perhaps I best not say any more," she finally said, "lest you think I'm as loony as you are."

I decided to put the insult aside for a moment and encourage her calmly.

"No such thing. I am eager to hear your story, so please tell it as you wish. I promise not to think you're crazy," I lied.

She gave me a doubtful look, chewed her lower lip a little more, but then continued anyway.

"If you say I'm potty, Percy St.-John, I'll find a stout stick to whack you."

"You have my word. I'll not say a thing against you. You're as sane as Cosmo here."

"Yes. Maggie's fright was only the first of several incidents, one more disturbing than the last. The next came only a day later, when one of my closest friends, Elizabeth, used the same lavatory. She was washing her hands in the bowl and as she looked up she saw in the mirror a man standing behind her. An old man with whiskers and dressed all in black. The same man!"

"And I suppose she screamed like a *banshee* and ran from the lavatory, howling like a gale from Atlantic."

"Not exactly. When she turned round to see the man, there was no one. She turned back to the mirror and saw nothing in it."

"Nothing?"

"Yes. Nothing. Not even her own image. That's when she ran from the lavatory screaming like a *banshee* with its hair on fire."

"And I suppose that stirred up another kerfuffle?"

"You guessed it Mr. Sherlock Holmes. Once again classrooms opened and girls rushed into the corridor and one of the mistresses went to check on the lavatory and once again found nothing. Especially, no old man."

"I suppose Elizabeth is not the sort of girl to have hallucinations, eh?"

Hannah jutted out her chin about four feet, with a bit of fire in her eyes.

"Certainly not. Elizabeth is the most sober of girls. Head's so level she can run a sack race with a stack of books balanced on it."

I leaned back in my chair and considered for a moment. I noticed Cosmo was frowning. Well, Cosmo's face is so scared-up and distorted that most people can't tell when he's smiling and frowning, but knowing him as I did, I could tell.

"Anything special about that lavatory?"

"No. Not at all. It is just the lavatory that's used by all the classes on the second storey of the school. Just like the one on the first floor."

"What else?"

"Two days later something happened to one of the mistresses. You can take it from me that that put the fear in everyone. Even the doubters."

"What happened?"

"There is a beautiful garden — a partly enclosed garden — at the school, on the west side. One morning the French mistress — Mademoiselle Langois — sat on a bench in the garden, reading and enjoying the cooling breeze that blew through the hedges. She was apparently so absorbed in her book that she didn't at first notice it."

"Notice what?" I asked eagerly.

She gave me a Hannah look. It's hard to describe, but it's the sort of look that says it would have been better for mankind if you had been strangled in the crib.

"Didn't notice that a man was standing behind her bench. A man in a black suit with whiskers and now with a walking stick."

"Did she confront him? Demand to know who he was and what he was doing in a girls' school?"

She gave me another disappointed frown.

"No fear! She jumped to her feet and ran as fast as she could to the Head Mistress's bureau, where they both rushed to the window that looks out on the garden. But by then, there was no one there."

"No doubt the testimony of one of the mistresses had some credibility."

"Exactly. Some doubted Maggie and Elizabeth, but soon every tongue in the school was repeating what had happened to Mademoiselle Langois."

"And?" I encouraged.

"Well, Mlle. Langois is French, you understand. She lacks that reserve which Mrs. Amberson's Academy for Girls likes to instill in English girls. She threw a fit. Didn't exactly fall to the floor and start chewing the rug, but refused to return to the school until the Head Mistress has called in the gendarmes to investigate."

"And she did, of course."

"Oh yes. Next day, two of the Metropolitan Police's finest showed up and looked the place over from stem to stern. They especially spent several minutes giving the lavatory a once over. And then they left to report they had found nothing, but that the copper in the neighborhood should spend more time eyeing the school for anything peculiar. I think they figure that some loon from off the street is wandering into the school to frighten the girls."

"And he did, I suppose. The policeman from the street."

"Yes. We saw a lot of him for a few days. And better still, Mlle. Langois decided to return and everything was as it had been, for about twenty minutes."

"Twenty minutes?"

"Well, really about two days. That's when the old bounder in the black suit showed up again, this time frightening a girl named Annie."

"Don't tell me. In the lavatory."

"I always said you have a good mind, Percy. If only you can learn to focus it more keenly."

"What happened to Annie?"

"She didn't actually make it into the lavatory to be frightened. She merely opened the door to go in and was confronted by the old man in the black suit, who she says 'hissed' at her and unleashed a 'terrible stink' from his mouth."

"What did the Headmistress make of that?"

"Mrs. Amberson is no dummy. By now she figured out that the damnable lavatory was the nasty old man's favorite haunt, so she ordered a padlock on the room and now everyone uses that lavatory on the first floor."

"And that has solved the problem?"

"So far. It's been four days since anyone sighted the foul blister and so it's going round that all that's necessary is to avoid the lavatory—I suppose until Mrs. Amberson can call in the bloomin' Archbishop of Canterbury to do a proper exorcism on the little room. Imagine that. Driving the evil spirits out of a dashed loo!"

I couldn't help myself. "Well, we all need one occasionally. Why not demons?"

I got another one of those Hannah looks. Then she fell silent.

2

"What do you think?" she finally asked.

"I think someone is having a good one on the girls at Mrs. Amberson's Academy, including the French Mistress. That's what I think. But tell me. What are the students saying? I'll wager there are a lot of ideas floating about."

"You said a mouthful there. The girls mainly think it's the spirit of Mrs. A's father. He made sacksfuls of money in the coal business, but unfortunately got a little sozzled with the brandy one night and wandered into the front of a hansom cab in Piccadilly. That was two years ago. Mrs. A took it hard, and the guessing is the old man is visiting her. Probably to assure her that there's plenty of good brandy where he is currently residing."

I paused to think what a lot of nonsense all that was, but then I considered that I had lately been talking to a guardian angel who looked like an ugly cat who'd been chewed up and rejected as unfit to be eaten by a goat. I decided to say nothing and fortunately it was just then that Mr. Finermann summoned Hannah to continue her home studies. She left, clearly thinking hard about what she had just told.

It was not until next afternoon that Hannah collared me again, to say more about the spirit of Mrs. A's father whose odd appearances were turning her school wrong side up.

Of course, I assumed she wished to have more of my wise and levelheaded opinions about the mysterious apparition. I was wrong. She had in mind a new plan to get me in deep trouble.

"Percy?" she said, her eyes narrowed and casting a sidelong glance toward the door, to make sure we were alone.

"Yes," I said, bracing for something.

"I've decided I must have a look at the lavatory, where the spirit seems to live."

"But you said Mrs. Albertson has locked it and no one is able to use it."

"That's right. So, I have to go there at night, when Mrs. Albertson is asleep and nowhere near the lavatory."

Well, there it was. The terrible something I was braced for, and just to hear it made my spine crawl, like a legion of ants was marching up and down it.

"You can't be serious. For one thing, if you are caught, you'll surely be expelled. Just think what your Grandpapa will say about that. He would be very disappointed in you."

She gave me a look that said I was being uncooperative.

"But I have a good plan and that's why I won't get caught."

"You said Mrs. Albertson has locked the lavatory door. How are you going to overcome that?

She frowned and then narrowed her eyes again.

"That's where you come in. I want you to go with me, to pick the locks that will get us into both the school and then the haunted loo. I won't get caught if you help me. After all, you have such wonderful lock-picking skills."

Flattery. I wasn't fooled. But somehow, I was not ready for her plan to involve me in her scheme — as an accessory. I gave the notion all the consideration it deserved, which was about five seconds.

"You can't be serious! It's bad enough that you're going to get caught and disappoint your Grandpapa, but now you want to get me caught and then fired from the best job I could ever want. You need one of those head doctors, my girl. And a good one at that."

"I take it your answer is 'No'."

"You take it correctly. No, no, and again NO! Just so you're clear on it, that means I won't do it."

She looked down at her hands and then sighed quietly.

"I knew you are a little loony, Percy, but I never figured you for a coward. An uncooperative, craven, lowdown poltroon. Well, I guess that's all that's to be said."

She waited for me to respond to the insults by changing my mind, but I decided to remain silent. Finally, after a few minutes, she said, "Well, I suppose that's the end of it."

I said nothing, as she rose to leave. When the door closed behind her, Cosmo gulped.

"Good for you lad!" he said gleefully. "For a moment there, I thought you would give in. I'm proud that you stood your ground."

I was thinking that I doubted that was 'an end to it'; Hannah had her faults, but giving up was not one of them. She would surely try another method to get her way.

That happened next evening, as I was trying not to throw up my dinner watching Cosmo finish off a tasty mouse. She entered my little room, and quietly closed the door behind her, listing to make sure her Grandpapa and Mrs. Wambly were well out of earshot.

"I suppose you've given it some thought. About helping me, that is."

"No. I haven't given it a single thought. Still not dumb enough to break into your school looking for the ghost of Mrs. A's dear old papa."

She smirked; then frowned.

"Well, then, I suppose I'll have to do it on my own. It will be more difficult, of course, but I can do it."

I should have ignored her, but I was sucker enough to ask.

"How do you propose to deal with those locks?"

She reached into a small bag she carried and drew out a screwdriver she had likely taken from the workbench. "I'll use this, of course. First, to break the building lock and then the lavatory lock. Won't be easy, but I am strong enough to do it."

I doubted that, but perhaps she was. And anyway, she was clearly going to try.

"Of course, when I'm gone, Mrs. Albertson will be able to tell someone broke in, but maybe she will assume it was the spirit who did it."

"You have obviously forgotten about the extra police surveillance that Mrs. A. has gotten, since reporting the troubles. While you are working on the lock —

making lots of noise I might add — the local copper will hear you, and he'll have you in shackles in about five minutes."

She frowned and gave it some thought. I'd finally made a fateful argument.

"You are right, Percy. All the more reason I wish I could persuade you to do the helpful thing and get me in the building, quietly. It would be ever so sweet of you, to save me like that. To save me from prison and hard labor."

I wasn't dumb enough to believe the sweet talk, either, but it was clear she was not to be talked out of it. I made one more try.

"No. I'd rather not be ever so sweet and save you from gaol. Think how you will feel when your Grandpapa comes down to the precinct to get you out. How ashamed he will be."

She seemed stymied by what I told her to consider. She said nothing for the longest while, but seemed lost in thought. Then she rose without saying another word and left.

"Good lad," Cosmo congratulated me. "She will continue thinking about your warning and will change her mind."

I had no such confidence myself. Hannah was one of the most stubborn people I'd ever encountered and I fully expected her to stick to her plan like a limpet on a ship's hull. The next day — a Thursday — I did not see Hannah until she returned from school. I was at the workbench alone, while Mr. Finermann was in his bureau, working on his accounts. When she sidled up to my workbench and sat on the other stool, I braced for something odd. I was not disappointed.

"You'll not guess what happened today in a thousand years," she said in her playful way.

"Oh? Maybe I'll wait for you to tell me."

"You will remember the locked lavatory?"

"Yes."

"It's still locked of course, but students passing it were whispering that they heard noises. The sound of scratching on the door. Like a cat was trying to get out."

I heard Cosmo sigh. *We are blamed for everything*, he moaned into my mind.

"Scratching? Did they run to Mrs. Albertson's?"

"Yes. And she came up to listen at the door."

"And?"

"Nothing. The scratching has stopped and she heard nothing. Later we learned she had credited it to girlish imagination. Nothing more."

"That sounds reasonable to me."

"No. The girls who heard it — there were three of them — are all levelheaded people — nothing loony about them. I believe they heard something, and that it had stopped — or maybe decided to stop — when Mrs. Albertson listened."

I gave it a bit of thought.

"Alright. Assuming the three girls are telling what they heard, what does it matter? How does it change anything?"

"Don't you see? It's just more evidence that something is going on in that loo. It confirms what was already seen," she added, now standing with her hands on her hips and a look on her face that said I was being dense.

I had to admit that she had a point, but worse still, I knew that it had convinced her even more to carry out her plan to investigate for herself.

"Alright. Suppose it does. Eventually, Mrs. A and the other mistresses will figure out what's happening — like maybe a water pipe."

She frowned again and put her hands back on her hips.

"Percy, you are refusing to see that there is something strange going on here. It seems I'm going to have to solve this mystery on my own, armed of course with all that I have learned from Mr. Sherlock Holmes. But, I am going to solve it. And when I do, you'll be sorry you weren't in on it with me."

She turned to leave and sadly I knew where she was going. She had slung over her shoulder that little bag with the screwdriver.

"Wait," I said reluctantly.

She hesitated with her hand on the door latch, but didn't turn round.

"Alright. I'll go. I know you won't be talked out of this, and I suppose you are less likely to be caught if I am there to open locks and guide you in what I know about breaking into places at night. Am I right that you have never broken into a building at night?"

"Well, no," she said turning and with a sullen tone in her voice.

Just as I thought.

"Come back at midnight. Be sure not to let your Grandpapa hear you. It will only take us a few minutes to get to the school."

3

Hannah opened my door at midnight, as I knew she would. I had taken the precaution to sleep with my clothes on.

"I cannot say that I advise this, my lad, but I know why you are doing it. Good luck," I heard Cosmo groan.

The Edgware Road was empty as we made our way toward the school. Not a sign of life, even a wayward dog or stray cat. No coppers either, I was pleased to note. However, as we neared the school, a policeman rounded the corner. Luckily I saw him before he noticed us, and we were able to duck into the doorway of a shop. We waited there, crouching breathlessly, as he passed and once more we were fortunate that he did not glance our way. When I was sure he'd moved well down the Edgware Road, we ventured out again and move quickly to the school.

Once out front of Mrs. Albertson's Academy, Hannah took over and guided me around to the back, where she knew there was a well-shielded service entrance. This entrance was also well away from Mrs. Albertson's own rooms in the school.

"This is the first door you need to open," she said, nodding toward the lock. I took out my little tools and went to work. Fortunately, it was a very old lock and proved easy to open.

I opened the door silently, and Hannah took the lead, guiding me first down a dimly lighted corridor and to a stairs at the end.

"This goes to the classrooms on the second storey," he whispered.

We moved up quietly. Well, as quietly as we could, considering that every dashed step groaned and squeaked. We finally reached another corridor and Hannah led me by my hand to a door about midway. She stopped to listen intently for any sound within. Nothing.

"The lavatory," she said, in a sinister whisper.

Once again I took out my little tools and went to work on a lock that seemed old and easy to open. It proved a little tougher than the previous lock, but after a few minutes I heard the reassuring click. Hannah lighted a candle from her sack, and I opened the door slowly.

We both gazed in, expecting to find something strange and perhaps painful. Instead, we found an ordinary loo, with a closet door to one side. I opened the door wider and we both ventured in slowly. Hannah left the door open, in case we had to run for it, I figured.

"Well," I said. "Here we are."

Hannah said nothing, but I heard her draw in a deep breath. In that same instant we both looked at the closet door.

"Not there yet," she said. "Got to open that one too."

I tried the door and found that it too was locked. Once more I went to work with my tools and soon managed the lock.

I opened the door slowly. All was dark. At least, at first. Then, as if someone had turned up a gas lamp, a bright light flashed before our eyes. For an instant, it blinded me, but my eyes adjusted quickly.

I heard Hannah gasp. Then, I saw it too.

"My God!" she exclaimed in a voice that was too loud.

From the light, as if from a fog, there emerged the tall, slender black figure of a man, wearing a tall hat. He came toward us as if walking from a distance, though he was in a small closet.

Hannah's hand grasped my arm, as she drew in another deep breath.

At that moment, the man's long, thin face came into view, and my heart leaped into my throat to see it. It was Reverend Lovecroft, carrying his birch rod and scowling like he intended to use it.

"Run, Hannah! Run!" I shouted. "And don't stop to look back."

She needed no further encouragement. As I turned to follow, my will was broken by the sound of a menacing voice from the closet.

"A word with you, Master St.-John. If you please," he said, in a voice filled with even more than his usual malice.

I couldn't tell you why even now, but instead of following Hannah I turned to hear him out. Perhaps I was somehow compelled to do so. I just don't know.

When I turned he was in full view, standing over me as he had so often before, and with that look that reminded my hands that pain was but a moment away. My scalp was tingling. My feet couldn't move.

"Why do you wish to avoid me, Master St.-John? Just a few weeks ago, you thought of nothing but me."

He smirked and then exhaled a hollow laugh.

I fell back against the frame of the open door.

"You must hear me out," he demanded. "I have important knowledge to impart to you, eh. "

Now he laughed heartily, as if remembering some wonderful joke. Meanwhile, I said nothing, but was sure I'd hear all he had to say. My feet were frozen in place and I knew that any attempt to run would fail, that I had no choice but to endure the terror.

"You are on the wrong side of this thing, Percival. May I call you Percival?" he smirked again.

"Or, rather, you are about to be. I have come to advise you to mind your own business. You are no match for us. If you persist, we will crush you like a worm under the boot."

I was just wondering what I was persisting in, when his eyes began to give a pale green glow. The glow quickly flashed into a kind of green fire, and it was then the aspect of Reverend Lovecroft dissolved entirely into a wolf-like creature, standing on his hind legs and snarling at me. His long tongue lashed about, dripping red saliva, or was it blood?

All this was frightening enough to overcome my paralysis. I turned and ran, not even bothering to close the door behind me. I dashed down the corridor, stumbled and slid down the stairs and then, thinking I must be pursued, limped to the entrance door.

There, I had the presence of mind to close and lock it behind me. As I backed away, certain that Lovecroft or whatever it was, would come blasting through after me, I withered to feel a hand on my shoulder. My heart jumped into my mouth and began beating on the back of my front teeth to get out. Then, a familiar voice whispered, 'Percy'. It was Hannah.

"What was that?" she gasped, as I was also trying to breathe again.

"What was what?" I asked, wondering if she had seen the same thing I had.

"The light from the closet. When I saw that, I took off."

"Do you mean to say you saw nothing but the light?"

"Yes. I thought you would be right behind me, but when I got here, you didn't come out. So, I decided to wait for you. I figured you were locking the door."

"No I didn't lock it. But never mind about the light. It was probably just a gas light that had been left on in the closet."

She seemed to accept my explanation, and I wasn't about to tell her about Lovecroft. She was already convinced that my mind was unsteady and that would leave no doubt of it. Besides, I was mainly convinced myself that I had had another of my terrifying imaginings.

CHAPTER FIFTEEN
WHEREIN THE BIG MAN ARRIVES

1

Making some sense of what had happened at the school occupied much of my thinking for the next few days. In due course, it all connected with my deep sense of having failed Arthur.

Was Lovecroft, as he appeared, a demon? Was he part of what Cosmo had meant by "there be demons in this place"? Could I never get justice for Arthur and "the others" because I was just not powerful enough to deal with such a creature as Lovecroft?

Or, more likely, was Lovecroft's appearance as a demon just my imagination making excuses for having failed Arthur? I finally decided it was this last. After all, at the school Hannah had seen nothing but a light. And, moreover, by this time I had plenty of evidence from my own experiences that my mind was playing tricks on me like a continuous magic show. Unfortunately, that put me back to zero. I had failed to do justice for Arthur and I had to figure out somehow to do so. I might have spent some time thinking about how to do that, but then reality intruded.

Aside from his rooms, Mr. Finermann maintained a small study just off the shop front, where he kept his accounts and filed his papers. I knew he kept his money at the bank across the Edgware Road and so I figured he did not keep much ready cash. He seldom asked me to help in his study and I never saw him invite a customer into that room until one day in early June a big man in a blue suit and bowler hat came in the shop and without a word between them followed Mr. Finermann into the study. The fellow had a round face with birdlike eyes and a large red beezer — it was a world champion among big red noses. I'd never seen him before, but Mr. Finermann clearly knew him and wished to have a word with him in private. At first I figured he must be a special customer — maybe wanting to order lots of locks. They spoke for most of an hour before the man left with only a nod to me.

I thought no more of the visitor until he returned the next week and once again, and without a word, followed Mr. Finermann into the study. This time I listened particularly for what was being said, but they both spoke in such undertones that I could not make it out, even with my ear close to the door. When the visitor left, Mr. Finermann remained in his study for a good long while but later said nothing to me about who the visitor was. I was left to guess what business he had with the shop.

A week passed with no more visits from the burly man with the red nose, and work — and learning — continued at a fast pace. I slept soundly every night, until one night when I suddenly awakened near midnight. I heard an odd sound in the workshop and at first thought; it must be Cosmo, chasing a mouse, but he wasn't. Without waking Cosmo, who still slept soundly, I rose carefully, put on my trousers, and cracked the door just a little. Nothing. So I moved into the workshop and to the door, which I also cracked and looked out. Then, I could see a figure that looked very much like Mr. Finermann, reach the end of the alley and turn into the Edgware Road. The man carried a bag, which resembled Mr. Finermann's tool bag, so I looked in the workshop and noticed that the tool bag was missing. *Could it have been him*, I wondered. I returned to my cot, but I lay awake for hours wondering if indeed Mr. Finermann had gone out. I had found the door locked, so it seemed likely it had been him and he had re-locked the door behind him. Why would a thief do that?

Finally, about daybreak — I figured it was about 6 o'clock — I heard the door open gently and then a soft footstep as Mr. Finermann climbed the stairs to his rooms. Then, only the usual silence of the shop.

That morning, as I puzzled about what had happened, it sprang into my mind that Mr. Finermann might have a lady friend. I gave that notion all the consideration it deserved and in about one-tenth of a second I heard Cosmo chortling that I must be stone cold BARMY.

"Aye. Why would Mr. Finermann need his tool bag to visit a lady friend, eh?" said Cosmo, as he continued his chortling, guffawing, and gurgling from under my cot. Didn't seem to me *angelic* to be making such noises.

I hesitated to ask Mr. Finermann about his goings and comings. It was his private business and not mine. If he had wanted me to know he would have taken the trouble to tell me. The proof that Mr. Finermann had gone out most of the night came that day. He was tired and the worse for his sleepless night. So was I.

I heard no more of such noises in the night for a week, but then it happened again. Mr. Finermann rose about midnight, left the shop, remembering to lock the door behind him, and then disappeared down the alley. Once again, though I took note of what had happened, I decided not to ask about it. I half decided that Mr. Finermann's 'private business' might be visits to a lady friend, after all. It puzzled me to think of Mr. Finermann as a romantic man, but I told myself that London was the sort of place where anything could happen. Then, *anything* did happen.

2

I worked hard to convince myself that Mr. Finermann's nighttime habits were none of my business, but it didn't work. My curiosity won out in the end and soon I had decided that next time he ventured out, I would follow and find out where he was going. That opportunity didn't come for quite a while. Not until Mr. Finermann had yet another visit from the big man with the red nose. Somehow, I had come to associate those visits and that man with Mr. Finermann's nighttime activities, and sure enough, a long meeting in the study was followed that very night, just after midnight, by another excursion to who knew where.

At the first sound of noises from Mr. Finermann's loft I roused myself and dressed. Soon Mr. Finermann came down and moved quickly out the alley door. As before, I cracked the door and watched him disappear down the alley, toward the Edgware Road. I followed, and by running some and dodging into shadows, I managed to keep Mr. Finermann in sight as he moved south toward Hyde Park and then further south into the area of London called Mayfair. A part of London where the rich and powerful folk live. *What is Mr. Finermann doing in Mayfair*, I wondered, as I followed cautiously at a distance? *Not likely to have a lady friend here*.

Moving down Park Lane and into Mayfair I saw no one but Mr. Finermann. He passed no one and neither did I. However, as I neared the end of my pursuit, a shadowy figure emerged from an impasse between large houses, and this sent me falling back into shadows to hide. It was the figure of a small man, who seemed to glance toward Mr. Finermann and then moved off in the same direction. Suddenly, I was following both this new shadow and Mr. Finermann.

Finally, the man followed Mr. Finermann as he turned into a street called Wood's Mews. I ran to catch up to see where they'd gone, but as I looked up the street, I saw only Mr. Finermann. No sign of the man. Mr. Finermann then stopped, as if thinking what to do or perhaps where to go. He seemed to be getting his bearings. I stopped also and watched, not wanting to chance being noticed by moving closer, but still wondering where the small man had gone. In a minute or two, Mr. Finermann moved up the street, now seeming to know where he was going.

Soon he stopped at an alley that ran between two high hedgerows that separated two large houses, each set in a considerable park, with lawns stretching for a great distance. He crouched behind one hedge, looking out across a lawn toward one of the big houses.

"Good Heavens," I whispered to myself, "it looks like he's doing a burglary!"

3

He continued to crouch and to watch for such a long while that I began to wonder what he was looking for. After a half-hour or so I got my answer. From the other end of the short street a large figure, also crouching while walking, moved toward Mr. Finermann. I could not see who it was, but the shape of the shadowy figure seemed similar to the burly man with the red nose who'd come to visit the shop.

The two converged and crouched together in the hedge. I could not tell for sure but it seemed they were whispering. After a few minutes, Mr. Finermann moved through the hedge and onto the lawn, followed by the big fellow. When both had gone, I moved forward quickly to the spot where they had crouched and looked through the hedge. I was just in time to see Mr. Finermann crawl through a window with his tool bag and into the darkened house, while the bulky man waited just outside, looking this way and that. For a moment I thought the big man might have seen me, but he turned his attention elsewhere. With him watching there was no hope that I could sneak through the hedge and get a closer look at what Mr. Finermann was doing in the house. I could see, however, that Mr. Finermann's entrance into the house did not cause any lights to go on, and so he was working in the dark.

While I watched I began to consider further that it sure looked like Mr. Finermann and his bulky accomplice were doing a burglary. This conclusion, however, ran hard up against my faith in Mr. Finermann as a solidly moral and even a religious man. I had observed him in his business and I knew him to be scrupulously truthful and honest with his customers. If he were a crook, surely I would have seen him cheating those very people. It just didn't make sense and so the more I thought about it the more confused I became. And yet, the evidence of a burglary was unfolding right before my eyes, complete with an accomplice who looked the part of a London thug if I knew my London thugs. I would have believed it if you told me he was Paddington Georgie's father.

In about half an hour Mr. Finermann handed his bag out the window and followed it, apparently unobserved by anyone in the house. He had something in his arms that I could not quite make out, but it looked like a small box. Unfortunately, I couldn't remain where I was because the two were advancing quickly across the lawn toward me, crouching and moving from the shadow of one tree to another. I retreated to where I had observed them before and waited for them to come through the hedge.

When they again stood in the Wood's Mews, the big man handed the bag to Mr. Finermann in exchange for the small box, and they parted, each in the direction by which he had come. Mr. Finermann walked toward me, so I thought it best to run quickly up to Park Lane and find a place to hide 'til he had passed. I figured he would head north toward the Edgware Road and home, and so he did. I dashed through Hyde Park and took a side street to get ahead of him. That was not hard to do, because Mr. Finermann, clearly tired, moved slowly.

As I turned into the Edgware Road I happened to catch sight of an unexpected shadow behind me — trailing at about twenty yards. At first I thought it must be a cat or dog or some critter, but then I knew — somehow — that it was a person. Was it the small figure I'd seen back at the Wood's Mews? I fell into a shop's doorway, hoping the shadow did not see me duck in. And there, I waited for it to pass.

In less than a minute the follower crept past, clearly confused that I was no longer in sight ahead. It was much smaller than I had expected, so I jumped out and took hold of it by both arms. When the shadow screamed, "Let me go!" I knew it was Hannah. An angry Hannah, in fact. The worst kind.

"What are you doing here?" I asked, stupidly, as she bit my hand. I stifled a howl and instead settled for a quiet grown and a curse word or two.

"What do you think I'm doing, silly? I'm following you and Grandpapa."

I did not care to risk waking the neighborhood by questioning her further on the street, or getting another bite. Still holding her arms we ducked into the alley and entered the shop by its back door. Once inside, she demanded again to be released. I gladly complied.

"Why were you following me?" I asked, wincing and holding my wounded hand.

"We don't have time for this," Hannah answered. "Grandpapa will be here in a minute. We'll talk in the morning."

She was right, of course, so I had no choice but to comply.

"Right. In the morning."

Tucked safely in my cot with Cosmo purring beside me, I heard the faint sounds of Mr. Finermann's return and then footsteps as he made his way slowly up to his rooms. I did not go to sleep soon, however, despite the fatigue of following him. My hand still ached and I was far too anxious about what I had seen. Why had Hannah followed us, and what would she have to tell in the morning? And, though I had denied it to myself, what I had seen had looked exactly like a burglary, and I for one knew what a midnight break-in should look like. Why would Mr. Finermann break into a house in the middle of the night except to rob it? When the answer to that question came — and I did not have long to wait — it changed my life forever.

PART THREE
THE MIDNIGHT BOY

CHAPTER SIXTEEN
WHEREIN I PURSUE MR. FINERMANN'S SECRET

1

The next morning, as we shared a bit of black bread and cheese, I found Mr. Finermann even less talkative than usual. Tired, I guessed. A sleepy-eyed Hannah had to depart for school and so I knew I'd not be able to question her further until she returned that afternoon. The late night and all that running had left me tired as well. Finally, at about noon Mr. Finermann excused himself, went up to his rooms, and though he didn't say so, I knew he needed a bit more sleep. Whatever he was doing out till all hours, I knew that Mr. Finermann was just too old and frail for that kind of work.

Meanwhile, I worried that Mr. Finermann was a thief, despite all my convictions about how honest he was. Then, I would decide that he could not be a thief and there must be another explanation for what I'd seen. All day and well into the next night I struggled with these contradictory thoughts and the harder I tried to resolve them, the more distressing and impossible they became.

The trouble was I could not know how to do that, short of asking Mr. Finermann what he was up to. I considered that, but then concluded once again I could not. I decided I would just have to wait for another chance, if ever one came.

The next morning, I was so quiet and distressed that Mr. Finermann — now much more alert — could tell that something was wrong. He did not question me at first, but later in the day he asked, "Percival... ." — He always called me by my given name — "Percival, are you feeling quite well? I only ask because you have seemed very quiet and possibly ill the past two days."

"Oh, I've been a little tired," I said, "Because I have had a restless sleep."

"And why is that?" he asked.

I thought that this must be the time to confront Mr. Finermann with what I'd see, but I could not bring myself to do so. It seemed to distrust Mr. Finermann —

following him like that — and I was sure he would be disappointed in me and might even tell me to leave his shop. I drew back and told a lie.

"I don't know why. Might be because Cosmo has been making noise-chasing mice. Not sure."

"Ah, yes. Quite so. He is quiet, but sometimes the mice excite him so." He smiled. "He's a good mouser. The best I've ever seen."

2

While Cosmo tended to endear himself with almost everyone, despite his looks, Mrs. Wambly clearly did not like him. She avoided him and, happy as she was otherwise, she always became glum and guarded when he was around. At first, I was puzzled about this, because I could not understand it, so I asked Mr. Finermann's opinion. I felt free to do so, because I saw one day that he noticed it too.

"That is not easy to tell, Percival," he answered, "but I believe Mrs. Wambly must be one of those rare people who have a fear of cats. I have heard that there is such a fear, as with people like me who have a fear of heights."

That made sense, and if you were afraid of cats, surely you would be terrified of a cat with a face like Cosmo's. Still, I wondered at what seemed to be Mrs. Wambly's peculiar dislike for him.

Meanwhile, I was soon able to question Hannah out of earshot of Mr. Finermann.

"Why were you following me the other night?" I finally asked her, as she helped me clean up the shop. At first, she seemed to remain sullen and unwilling to respond. But then she relented.

"I also heard Grandpapa, and it worried me to think what danger he might be in — going out so late at night. I'd noticed him go out before and I've been concerned about him — you know, that he might be harmed."

"Well, what did you see and what did you conclude from it?" I asked.

"I didn't see much of anything. I followed you and had to stop a distance from you because I didn't want to be seen. So, I don't know where Grandpapa and the big fellow went, once they disappeared into the hedges. Where did they go?"

I fell into a thoughtful silence.

"I guess it won't do any harm to tell you, now that you know most of it anyway," I agreed. "Mr. Finermann and the big man broke into a dark house. While your Grandpapa went through the window, the big man kept watch. When Mr. Finermann came out, carrying his tools and a box, they returned. You saw the big man leave by coach, while your Grandpapa walked home by the same way he'd come."

"But what does it all mean?" she asked, in an anxious voice. I paused again, concerned about what I could say to her without unleashing a volcano.

"I'm not sure," I said, but it doesn't look good.

Hannah frowned. "You think Grandpapa robbed the house, don't you? I can see it in your eyes," she demanded, glaring at me. I saw Cosmo take cover under a workbench. "You are mistaken," she continued, now beginning to tear. "Grandpapa is an honest man! He is a good man! He would never steal from anyone. Never. Not even if he was starving," she insisted.

"Hannah, you are mistaken yourself. I do not believe Mr. Finermann is a thief. Not at all. I know he is a good man. An honest man. But still, we don't know what is going on. Why would he go out in the middle of the night and enter dark houses through a window?"

She gave me a disbelieving look.

"You are lying, Percy. You DO believe Grandpapa is a thief. I'll tell you what is going on and I'll use short words so even you can understand. Grandpapa is somehow being forced by the fat man with the pink face to rob places for him. Forced," she repeated. "Everyone knows that in the detective novels the big man with the fat face is always an unspeakable fiend of some kind. It's a distinguishing feature of the breed, eh."

"I am not lying to you," I assured, taking her hand. "We are going to discover what is going on. And maybe Mr. Finermann *is* being forced, as you believe. But, whatever is going on, I need your help."

"How?" she asked, her head tilted to one side, her narrow eyes looking out at me from under the overhang of a doubtful frown.

"I know you haven't asked your Grandpapa about his nighttime activities, else you would not have followed that night. Is that right?"

"Yes. I didn't have the nerve to ask him. I was afraid of what he would say if I was curious. So, I kept my silence."

"Good. Continue to do that, and now you can join me as we find out what this is all about. What's going on with the big man and the nighttime house breaking?"

She gave me another hard look, but then smiled.

"Alright. I agree. But you must promise to let me go with you when you follow again," she said with an assertive frown.

"It's a bargain," I said, smiling. "We are a team."

Then she smiled again, only this time with conviction. I noticed Cosmo peer out from under the workbench.

3

In the next weeks, there was no occasion to follow Mr. Finermann, so it seemed my secret fear that I might not have another chance to observe him was coming true. No sign of the big man, and life at the shop proceeded as usual. Meanwhile, Mr. Finermann continued to teach me the finer points of opening safes and vaults, both with tools of various kinds and by the subtle art of listening to the inner workings of the safe locks. He even introduced me to a new tool, which he had made, based on thinking of someone named Tesla — a device that connected by wires to a storage battery of the kind that the new electric torches used and to a little meter that could tell him of the subtle movements of parts of the lock. It was fascinating and I learned it as best I could.

"Never think that you can know the combination in advance," he warned me. "People will set a combination according to some numbers that are important to them in their lives — a birthday, for example — but even if you know the person well, you'll not be able to guess such a number. Forget that kind of reasoning. It's a fool's game and wastes time."

And if you are breaking into safes in the middle of the night in a stranger's house, I thought to myself, *you certainly have no time to waste.*

"Is there some standard way of setting the turning of the combination wheel? Left-Right-Left, for example? And a set number of numbers? Three? Four?"

"No. It depends on the safe's manufacturer. If you see a Miller Safe, for example, you will know that the manufacturer advises four numbers, while an Enos Wilder Safe fixes the number at only three. And both let you set them in any direction and order. Some safes are pre-set in that fashion and only ask the buyer to decide upon the combination. I sell some safes to people who ask me to set both! But remember this, Percival. Every safe can be opened by someone who does not know the combination in advance if he is skilled enough to do so. Every safe," he repeated.

On the days that we made locks I showed that I excelled at this trade, and Mr. Finermann complimented me for it. "You are becoming a fine locksmith, my boy, and I do not doubt that one day you will exceed even me."

As the days passed I remained convinced that Hannah and I would have another opportunity to follow Mr. Finermann on one of his nighttime outings. My curiosity about those strange activities sometimes troubled my mind, especially as I lay in my cot at night, not knowing if I would hear him leave the shop. I confess that I also worried that Hannah would change her mind and ask Mr. Finermann about the matter. I considered that there seemed no way to escape the conclusion that Mr. Finermann was up to no good.

Meanwhile, I tried not to be preoccupied about it and I was able to act quite normally, so Mr. Finermann had no concerns about what was "the matter" with me. Things went as usual.

Sometime later, I shared with Hannah a theory that troubled me, though I knew it might frighten her.

"I think there's a chance that the big man is somehow forcing Mr. Finermann to work for him by holding something over his head. Maybe the thugs have threatened to kidnap you or harm you, if he does not help them."

"That's a sound idea, Percy," said Hannah. "You may be onto something. Dear Grandpapa would do anything rather than see me in danger." We said no more about it.

To me that explained all the facts — how an otherwise honest man could be compelled to do something dishonest — like burglary.

Then, one day I had another idea, which I put to Hannah. "Following Mr. Finermann will only show us what we already know. He goes in the middle of the night to houses and breaks into them, probably to rob safes. And in the nighttime robberies, the big man is an accomplice, first by coming to the shop and then by meeting Mr. Finermann at the site of the robbery, where he acts as lookout and assistant."

"Yes. That appears to sum-up what we know," she agreed.

"So, next time the big man comes, when he leaves I will follow him and learn more about *him*. Maybe that will tell us much more about what Mr. Finermann is up to. Maybe."

I had expected my excellent idea to cause Hannah to brighten and flail about with indescribable joy, but instead she stomped all over it with hobnail boots. Her face darkened and she frowned.

"You are going to follow. It sounds like you are going to follow without me."

"Yes. I fear so. The big man is likely to leave by cab or coach and I'll have to use our bicycle to follow. And, if I have to follow him a great distance, there's no way I have the stamina to do so with you on the handlebar."

She pondered a moment, and then let the frown fade from her face.

"Very well, but you must pledge to tell me all you discover. Nothing held back, eh."

"Agreed."

CHAPTER SEVENTEEN
WHEREIN I FOLLOW THE BIG RED NOSE

1

Once I had decided to follow the big man and how I would do it, he did not come. Weeks passed — no sign of him. It was as if my eagerness for him to come was keeping him away. I took the opportunity to practice my skills on the bicycle. Then one day, he suddenly entered the shop. Hannah, just home from school, and I said nothing, but exchanged faint smiles. Without a word, Mr. Finermann directed him into the study. Before he closed the study door, I asked after Mr. Finermann if I could have the rest of the day to myself, to do some personal business. He nodded and that was my signal to finish my work at the bench and hurry to the alley where we kept the bicycle. In a minute or two I was on the walkway across the Edgware Road, watching eagerly for the big man to exit the shop. No coach or cab was waiting so I assumed he would leave on foot, but which way would he go? Perhaps toward me. I hid as well as possible, considering the bicycle.

As in the past, after an hour or so the big man emerged from the shop and walked up the street in the other direction. I followed, slowly pushing the bicycle on the walkway. He turned the corner. I hurried to keep him in sight and just as I turned the same corner I saw him boarding a coach. I hopped on the bicycle and followed at a distance.

It was not difficult to keep pace with the coach. At the time of day, especially, the streets of London were busy with wagons, coaches, carriages, motors and even a few bicycles like mine. I kept my distance and followed.

The coach took me down the Edgware Road to the Park and then east toward central London. I was tired keeping up but I persisted, thinking he must stop soon. He didn't.

I followed as the coach turned south toward the River. I was so tired I was starting to loose my pace, but something made me quicken my effort. The coach turned out Whitechapel Road and then south again toward the Docks.

"Yes!" I shouted to myself. Exactly where I expected the thug to go. Finally, the coach turned into a narrow street just off the Victoria Warf, oddly enough named Narrow Street. *Londoners don't use much imagination in naming streets*, I thought. Drab shops lined one side of the street, while on the other stood a large dreary building with a sign out front saying London Water and Sewers Authority.

2

The coach stopped at a tobacconist's shop. It was a big shop. I waited while the red beezer alighted and entered the shop, I guessed to buy tobacco. Meanwhile, the coach moved on. Twenty minutes passed. I waited and watched. No sign of the big man. Finally, I began to feel conspicuous, just waiting and watching the shop, and I was concerned that I must return to the lock shop before nightfall. After an hour I had no more time to linger and wait for the big man's coach to return, so I reluctantly turned my bicycle and peddled west toward Paddington.

As I peddled homeward I considered how the big man's destination — the tobacco shop near the Docks — was just the sort of place a gang of thugs would call home — where any self-respecting scrum of London criminals would wish to make their headquarters. Probably eating opium in the shop's basement I told myself.

I arrived at the lock shop well after nightfall. Mr. Finermann was curious.

"Where was it you had to go in such a hurry, Percival? And why so late?" he asked, seemingly concerned that something might be the matter.

"Just an errand that my old landlord asked me to do for her," I lied. "Took longer than I expected."

He nodded as if he believed me but did not want to intrude any further. Just after he went up to his rooms to have his dinner and then to bed. I took some bread and cheese from my food drawer and dined as I usually did. Of course, it was insufficient for Cosmo, so he asked to go into the alley and hunt for rats. Just as I finished, Hannah barged in.

I quickly told her were the big man had gone.

"Well, it seems Mr. Finermann has somehow fallen under the power of criminals. It's unthinkable that he would willingly be in league with them and yet he is working with them for sure. Somehow — right in our faces — he is involved with such people."

Hannah neither agreed nor opposed, and finally left for her room. As I continued to consider the issues it all came down to a brutal question. Why was Mr. Finermann doing crimes in company with a thug? What was it they were holding over him, assuming he would not willingly help them?

As I lay in my cot that night, I continued to think about the big man's destination, until I finally drifted to sleep.

Morning brought no clarity to my confusion. I mulled the thing over all day and by closing time I'd concluded there was only one way to resolve my questions — to ask. I knew that I could persuade Mr. Finermann to tell me what he was all about — his association with the big man and his midnight rambling. The trouble, however, was that to do that, I would have to admit I had followed him and that I had done the same with the big man. That could be a problem. Embarrassing in the least. Perhaps angering at worst. Surely, Mr. Finermann would be disappointed in me — which I had followed him and suspected him. These worries stopped me cold.

I worked at my bench, but thinking of the thug.

"You best mind your own business entirely," Cosmo suddenly interrupted into my mind. "You're going to make the old man angry and get us thrown out of here and then where will we be? Back to eating roaches in some forsaken basement. That's where!" he huffed.

Somehow, Cosmo's worries about diet did not rate very high on my list of concerns. I was far more interested in the big man's identity.

3

Then it occurred to me. The big man had come as in the past, but that night Mr. Finermann had not gone out at midnight, as he had so far done after each visit from the big man. *Why not?* I wondered. My answer came in the afternoon, just before closing.

The big man returned, this time accompanied by two others. Hannah sat in a corner; nose buried in her sketchbook and seemed at first not even to notice the arrivals. Then she gave me a knowing look. The big man's two companions looked like silver-ring bookmakers, with nicely trimmed side-whiskers and bowler hats. Perhaps I was just suspicious, but all three faces had deep frowns. I continued my work at the bench, as the three followed Mr. Finermann into his study. It seemed to me that he too looked worried.

They were in there a long time — longer than usual it seemed. "Why were they worried? Were they all three from the gang, or syndicate?" I whispered to Hannah.

I stayed close at the workbench during the long meeting, trying my best to repair a lock while my mind was completely distracted by thoughts of what was going on and especially what was the matter. I hoped Mr. Finermann was not in some trouble or worse yet, in some danger. Beyond every other worry I had managed to conjure up in my mind, I continued to fret that he was simply too old and frail to be breaking into houses at midnight, no matter his reasons. I had done it myself and so I knew what it took to shoulder the strain.

Hannah ventured over to the study door, straining an ear to hear what was being said inside. "No good," she lamented as she returned to the sketching. "Not a sound. I think they're whispering. Otherwise I'd have heard them." Now, however, Hannah moved over to my workbench and took a seat next to me, watching closely what I was doing.

Finally, time to close the shop rolled round and the four had not yet emerged from the study. I decided to lock the door and hang out the Closed sign on my initiative. Still, Hannah and I remained at the workbench. I wanted to see all the faces when they emerged.

Within the half-hour, the door opened and the visitors walked out first. They all looked even more anxious than before. When Mr. Finermann came behind them, his face was so drawn that it unnerved me for a moment. The gents walked out and up the Edgware Road without good-bye and Mr. Finermann turned and went up to his rooms without a word to us.

'Something's amiss," said Hannah, shaking her head. "We must discover what it is."

I said nothing but nodded.

That night, as I lay in my cot, my thoughts bounced between my fear of what Mr. Finermann had gotten himself into and my continuing sadness that I had failed Arthur. This last was never far from my mind and much as I thought about it, I could think of no way to make good on that promise to Arthur and myself.

CHAPTER EIGHTEEN
WHEREIN CHILDE PERCY TO THE DARK TOWER CAME

1

All the way home from following the big man I had one thought in my head that I could not shake. *What was in that tobacco shop that was so attractive to the big man?* I considered that it must be the headquarters of the gang that somehow had Mr. Finermann in its clutches. Maybe I thought it was merely the business that the big man owned and his presence there for such a long time was completely unremarkable. True, all the while I watched I saw no one else enter the shop, but then I had not had time enough to watch to be sure of anything and of course I could not watch the rear entrance while keeping an eye on the front.

From all this thinking during my long ride home and more such thinking in the following days, it was but a short step to deciding that I must have a look inside the shop to know for sure about the big man. I suppose it was a natural decision for a picklock and safeman to make, and within a short while I was wondering when I could get away and break into the tobacco shop.

Hannah seemed to be thinking along the same lines, but I was troubled to know that she would surely want to go with me. Still, one of us needed to remain at the shop in case something unexpected happened during the night.

Hannah gave a reluctant nod to my plan and to staying behind, but I feared she would follow me anyway, across London in the middle of the night on her own and into that terrible neighborhood.

Just before retiring that evening I took Hannah aside and gave it one more time to assure her agreement with my plan. I noticed that Cosmo was listening attentively. I explained my reasoning and determination to Hannah and of course she had changed her mind and insisted on going with me.

"Trouble is, we have only one bicycle, and I'm not about to peddle you all the way across London on the handlebar. Only one of us can go and that's got to be me."

"I don't like it, Percy. You are going to get yourself in trouble and there'll be no one there to help. I'll worry the whole while you are gone."

"I would do the same, Hannah. It can't be helped. I need you to keep an eye on things here. After all, we don't know that Mr. Finermann won't go out on one of his break-ins tonight and if so you'll have to follow and see what he does. We have to be able to cover both issues at once."

The stone cold logic of this last persuaded Hannah to stay behind. No sidestepping the fact that someone needed to keep an eye on her Grandpapa and make sure he had help if he got himself in a mess.

That night, when all was quiet for an hour upstairs, I rose, dressed, and opened the door an inch to make sure no one was in the shop.

Once on my bicycle and gliding down the Edgware Road I was overcome with the dreadful reality that I was on a very dangerous mission. I was determined to go into what seemed to be the headquarters of the thugs, who I was convinced, had Mr. Finermann somehow in their grip and were forcing him to do burglaries for them. All my past experiences in breaking into places — shops and other buildings — seemed to pale in comparison to this night's danger.

Still, I peddled on, turning east toward central London and then — after an hour of hard riding — into Limehouse and south toward the docks. All the while with feelings of ever greater danger.

I stood for a long while beside the bicycle and in the shadows of a doorway, watching the tobacco shop for any sign of life. It was deathly still and quiet. Not a flicker of light or anyone on the street out front. I was utterly alone, it seemed. And as I stood there, looking up at the dark façade of the shop, I recalled the grim foreboding in a line from a poem of Browning's that was a favorite of my Father's. "Childe Roland to the dark tower came."

2

Soon, I began to wonder what was around back of the thing. *If the thugs were in there, they would probably come and go through the back and especially at this time of night*, I told myself. I peddled down the street and at the first corner turned to find an alley, if there was one. There was, and so I stopped and watched. Nothing.

Except for newspaper blowing about there was nothing to be heard or seen and particularly no one coming and going from a back door.

Then it hit me. If the thugs were in the shop, they might well be sleeping at this time of day. Somehow, the dubious notion that thugs would choose to sleep in a tobacco shop rather than wherever they called home did not hold much weight. I was now sure there were about fifty villains sleeping in that shop and the fact that the shop clearly had one upper storey tended to confirm my conviction. I proceeded with caution, having already decided that it would be safest for me to break in through the rear door.

I stored the bicycle in a nearby doorway and making sure I was indeed at the back door of the tobacco shop — remembering the mistake I had made with Mr. Finermann — I lighted my candle and took a look at the lock. It was old and easy. Nothing special there.

Working my little tools I opened the lock in about five seconds and eased the door open a few inches to peer in. The shop's back was entirely dark and I could see nothing. I decided I had not come all that way just to turn and run now, so I ventured in.

Holding high my candle I could see that I was standing in a storeroom of sorts, with boxes, crates, shelves, cleaning materials and tools and an old sort of coal burning stove. Nothing out of the ordinary I concluded. Especially, no sleeping thugs. I stood for a while, listening closely for any noise — no matter how faint — within the shop. Nothing.

Moving around the storeroom, I noticed a door, which I figured was a closet. I opened it and looked in to see two stairs, one leading down to a basement and one leading up to the second floor. I decided to put my fortune in God's hands, as my father would have suggested, and ascend to the second storey, where I would find a thug's dormitory if there was one.

The stairs creaked, of course, so I was sure anyone would hear me coming. Still I climbed to a door at the top. It was unlocked and so I opened it slowly enough to cast a little light inside. The more light my candle cast the more I could see that the second floor was an attic, full of junk. In fact, cluttered from floor to ceiling with all sorts of things, from old furniture to boxes full of pots, pans, crockery, plates, clothing, books and just about anything that a frugal person would store in the attic and forget about it. But whatever was stored there, it did not include a collection of used thugs.

I moved back onto the stairs and instead of stopping at the first floor storeroom I continued down to the basement. As I descended a stink that I had noticed all the while got much stronger. There was something dead and decaying in the basement. At the bottom of the stairs the stink was almost unbearable. I had arrived just in time to get its full force.

Again holding high my candle I surveyed the whole room from the stairs. Nothing seemed out of order, though there was much less stored in the basement than in the attic. On one wall there was a long rustic bench. In the middle of the room a long crate. And on the other facing wall a large cabinet. The other two walls had shelves with all sorts of jars and vases on them. For tobacco, I guessed.

At first I gave the wall with the bench a good look but found nothing of interest, except that the bench reminded me of a church pew. Then, as I turned to survey the wall with the cabinet, I noticed that the horrible stink suddenly faded, to be replaced by what was unmistakably the pleasant odor of lavender. The moment I started puzzling about that my candle suddenly went out and then all hell broke loose at once. Yes. Hell.

As I faced the wall with the cabinet and searched my pocket for a match to relight my candle, a great green glow suddenly illuminated the room, such that I could see my shadow cast on the cabinet wall. Realizing that the light was coming from behind me, I turned with a start and that's when I saw them.

I'm sure my mouth gaped about six inches and I rocked back onto the crate. There, sitting on the long bench were five men. They were all identical, all excessively thin and bald, and all of them green and glowing. Their ears, eyes and mouths were very large and their faces long and expressionless. They all looked at me.

My heart started leaping around in my chest, making its way to my mouth where it could escape. Then the five men stood and I realized for the first time that they were all not only tall, gaunt, and green, they were also naked. Not a stich on them, and as I look them top to bottom I saw that each had frog feet — enormous frog feet!

They stood and glared menacingly at me for the longest time, as if they were considering that I might be a tasty idea for dinner. Then without moving they all began to talk at me all at once. Though their speech was so jumbled I could not tell exactly what they were screaming at me, I knew they were all cursing me and condemning me to Hell. When they stopped their chatter all at once, the green man in the center — by now I recognized them from their evil faces as demons — began to address me in a very measured but evil voice.

"Percival," he called out slowly.

I decided not to answer, because I was thinking they were all a product of my diseased imagination and if I said anything to them it would only make things worse.

"Percival!" he then screamed, not to be ignored.

"Yes."

"We know you. We have observed you for quite some time, now," he said in a hollow, menacing voice. The others laughed and nodded among themselves.

"Yes?" I said.

"We've drawn you here to warn you — the only time we shall do so — that you must cease your harassment of us. You must stop your threatening interest in our friend Tobias and what he is doing. You must stop."

Somehow it did not surprise me to hear his warning but I staggered — if someone sitting on a crate can be said to stagger — to hear him call Mr. Finermann a "friend".

"Yes?" I repeated.

The five continued to glare at me with particular hatred, it seemed, and as they did so, I noticed the awful stink began to reemerge. Just then, however, the tall men — all of them taller than the big man — resumed their seats on the bench and immediately began to shrink and to shrivel, first to the size of dwarfs and then they dissolved into a green mist, which soon disappeared entirely.

I sat there, on my crate and in the dark, staring toward the wall, trying to console myself that my mind was so distorted that it would play such a trick on me. But then I realized that I was shaking uncontrollably with the terror I had felt at first seeing the green men. The demons. In fact, I was frozen in terror and though I wanted desperately to make for the stairs, I could not.

It wasn't easy to reconcile myself to sit where I was until I had managed to calm down, but I had no choice but to make the mental bargain. In five minutes or so I knew I could run up the stairs. It was the work of a minute or two to exit the back door and lock it behind me.

3

Though I was exhausted from my fright, I had no trouble summoning up the energy to peddle like my life depended on it, flaying through Limehouse and into central London. All the while my thoughts bounced back and forth between the conviction that my mind was again playing tricks on me — now even worse tricks — and the certainty that what I'd seen was real. By the time I reached the lock shop I had made no headway at all in resolving the dispute. But I was exhausted from both the long ride and the emotions of what I had observed, or thought I observed.

Hannah was waiting for me just outside my closet.

"What did you find at the tobacco shop?" she whispered.

I had no heart to sit up all night explaining the green demons to Hannah, and I certainly wasn't going to tell her the green men called Mr. Finermann their "friend". So, I brushed by her, saying, "Got to sleep now, Hannah. I'll explain tomorrow."

She did not make a ruckus outside my door, so I fell into a deep sleep.

I had no opportunity to speak with Hannah next day. She was gone before I got to my workbench in the morning and when she came home, Mrs. Wambly put her to work immediately at her chores. That gave me time to decide there was no way I would tell her about the green demons. She already thought I was at least a little barmy and I was half convinced she was right. At the very least, I knew that stories about demons would only cause her to go around the bloody bend and would cause me more grief.

Next day, Saturday, we decided to take our bicycle down to the park and take turns riding. We glided down toward the Marble Arch corner, with Hannah on the handlebars as usual, all the while cautioning me about going too fast and not watching where I was going.

After an hour of riding about the park on such a beautiful day, my mind was much more at rest than it had been in some time, though I reflected that I had learned absolutely nothing about the Big Man by my harrowing examination of the tobacco shop. I wonder what I — well, Hannah and I — would do next.

As we rested on a bench in the park, surrounded by beautiful tulips, I knew Hannah would finally want to know what happened at the tobacco shop. I was right.

"Percy," she said quietly, "you have not told me about the tobacco shop. Did you find evidence of the Big Man's gang? Were the thugs there, as we thought?"

"No. That's the dashed awful thing about it. I found not a living soul." I consoled myself that I was at least technically telling the truth.

"No one? Not even the tobacconist?"

"I searched all the floors, including the basement. Not a soul."

"Well, then, where are we?"

I considered for a bit.

"Not sure. We have the mysterious Big Man, and we can follow him. Or, we can wait for him to reappear and see if your Grandpapa does anything in response. I favor just observing and then responding to what happens."

The look on her face told me she inclined to agree, but she said nothing for the longest while. As unsure of things as I was, I figured. Then, she took my hand and when she spoke it was on an entirely new subject, almost as frightening as the tobacco shop. For some reason I decided to stand, while she remained seated on the bench.

"Percy."

"Yes."

"I've decided."

"What? Decided what?"

She paused again, pursing her lips and frowning.

"Oh, nothing."

I said nothing. Then she decided to continue.

"I... I've decided that I am going to marry you."

I gurgled, reeled a bit, and then gave at the knees. I decided to sit.

"Not now, of course," she quickly explained. "Only after I have finished at Beaux Arts and have established myself as a great artist."

I was still speechless.

"You'll have to move to Paris, of course, because that's where artists go, you understand. Perhaps Grandpapa will help you start your own shop there."

I did not reply, but I remember smiling and gurgling stupidly, as if she'd had a fine idea.

"Then too, you'll have to get your mind in what you might call normal condition. At the moment, you're still a bit of a loon and therefore not suitable for marriage. However, I'm sure you can make the effort and... well... get less potty. If you know what I mean."

As she continued to speak about working hard to make something of me I continued my silence and smiled rather like the lunatic she seemed to think I was. In a minute or two, Hannah decided she wanted to take another turn around the park on the bicycle, so I remained on the bench, staring blankly into the middle distance at nothing much.

When I came to my senses it was to acknowledge what a hideous thug Fate can be.

Well, there you have it, I moaned to myself. *First, I'm frightened out of my wits by tall green demons with giant frog feet, and now I must cope with a future married to one of England's supreme pills.* I wondered if life could get more painful. I was about to find out that it could.

CHAPTER NINETEEN
WHEREIN I FIND LOCKED SAFES AND BROKEN BONES

1

Later, at the shop, I put Cosmo out for his evening's hunt and took to my cot, fully dressed and listening closely for feet on the stairs. It suddenly struck me as odd that neither Mr. Finermann nor Hannah had gone to synagogue that weekend.

Finally, Mr. Finermann did not disappoint. At about midnight he descended the stairs and left, locking the back door behind him. I waited a moment, and then sprang from my cot and followed at a distance, making sure I remained unseen.

I don't know why but I suddenly had the feeling of being followed myself. Was it a shadow behind me, or just my imagination? I fell into an overarching doorway, and stopped breathing. Very soon the shadow proved to be real and came up the street behind me. As it passed the door, I sprang. It was then a familiar voice said, "Hey, what's all the rough stuff?" Then Hannah took a swing at me, clearly meaning to connect. Luckily I managed to dodge her fist, but only by an inch.

"What are you doing here?" I asked — a really dumb question I considered on reflection.

"Following," she said. "Same as you. And why didn't you wait for me? We're supposed to be in this together, eh? We better get onto it, or Grandpapa will lose us."

With no more useless questions about Hannah's presence, we once again followed, running to catch up as Mr. Finermann walked south, carrying his tool bag, toward Hyde Park Corner. As I thought, he was so slow that we soon found him. This time however instead of proceeding further south down Park Lane, he turned right into a street called Sussex Gardens and proceeded far to the southwest, almost to Lancaster Gate and the Park. There he stopped at a coach, drawn-up under a street lamp and at the side of the road. Out stepped the big man, alone this time as in the past. The two proceed up a side street to the north, toward Paddington Station.

"Could they be going to board a train?" Hannah asked.

Just then, however, they stopped well short of the Station, and for a moment surveyed a large house, set in a considerable park, which was entirely dark. Not a light shown. For a long moment, the two seemed to confer. Then as before, the big man kept watch, while Mr. Finermann proceeded alone, moving from tree to tree to hedges across the lawn to hide his advance toward the house. As he crouched and moved slowly across the lawn I wondered why anyone would use a man as old and frail as Mr. Finermann to do such work?

All the while Hannah clutched at my left arm, watching her Grandpapa's movements and probably wondering the same thing as me.

2

As in the past, the house remained entirely dark and my perspective was good enough to see that Mr. Finermann quickly opened a door and entered. From then, I could only speculate. I watched both the door and the big man who was peering through the hedge toward the house, doubtless watching for what was happening inside. Like us, he was probably waiting for Mr. Finermann to emerge and make his way back across the lawn.

Just then, however, a light went on in the house, and then another and another, until the entire building was aglow. It seemed that every window was now lighted and it didn't take much imagination to know that Mr. Finermann had been caught by whoever turned on the lights.

I didn't know why, but the big man was suddenly nowhere in sight. I guessed that for some reason he had returned to bring up the coach. Or, maybe he had just abandoned Mr. Finermann and had run away. So, it was up to Hannah and me. We dashed across the lawn and toward the door as fast as we could, not bothering to stop behind trees. When we reached the house we began to look in the windows, to see what we could. At the third window, we beheld a terrible sight. Mr. Finermann stood by a desk with his hands high in the air, while two men — rough-looking villains — pointed pistols in his direction. It did not appear that they were speaking — just holding the old man at bay. He had an agonized look on his face, as if he was already in pain.

Hannah could see it too. She gasped, but lucky for us stifled a scream. I quickly ran back to the door. She followed.

"Wait here. I'll be right back," I told her.

I entered, and made a racket, figuring that one or both of the gunmen would come to see what the matter was. I quickly ran back out the door, where I'd seen a shovel and hoe leaning against the house. I handed the hoe to Hannah and took up the shovel myself, and there we stood beside the open door waiting for anyone to come out. Soon, a man with a pistol emerged, and when he was clear of the door Hannah and I brought down the hoe and shovel on his head in unison and as hard as we could. That turned out to be very hard, because he fell in a heap, dropping his pistol as he went. Just then, of course, Hannah gave him another whack for good measure. I took up the pistol, ran back to the window, followed by Hannah, where I could see that one man remained with his pistol trained on Mr. Finermann but with a worried look and glancing at the door eagerly for his friend to return.

Suddenly I froze. Hannah saw that something was wrong.

"What?" she whispered. "Shoot him."

"I don't know how," I said.

"What? You don't know how to shoot?"

"No. I have never shot a pistol. Never even seen someone shoot one. Brixley, my village, is not exactly awash with pistols."

"Look. That's the hammer. Pull it back."

I did as she said.

"That's the trigger. Point that damn thing at the villain with the pistol and pull it with your finger."

"How do you know so much about pistols," I asked, doubtfully. She gave me a sympathetic look.

"The detective novels, of course. They're full of useful information about shooting people."

I decided to believe her. I aimed at the biggest part of the thug — his midsection — closed my eyes, and shot him through the window, hoping the bullet landed where I'd aimed. When the smoke and broken glass from the explosion cleared, I could see the blister on the floor, screaming about his knee. Apparently, my bullet had gone through both knees and the fellow was having quite a time of it. I had missed my target by a bit.

"You got the bastard!" Hannah yelled. Screaming with savage delight. 'Shoot him again!"

We ran back to the door, assured ourselves the senseless man was still at rest, and then ran into the house and toward where I figured Mr. Finermann could be found. When we burst into the room, the thug still screaming on the floor and Mr. Finermann staring at him, his mouth agape in disbelief.

Now I could see that Mr. Finermann had been banged up a bit by the gunmen, and was holding his right arm with his left hand.

"I believe they broke my arm," he winced, his eyes full of pain.

"Let's go," I said, taking his good arm and pulling toward the door.

"No," he protested. "I must open the safe."

"What safe?" I asked, looking around the room and still tugging at his arm.

"In there," he said, nodding toward what looked to be a closet door. "Probably in there. I must open it."

"You're in no shape to open anything," I said. "Besides, others might arrive at any moment and we'll be a couple of dead cracksmen. Think about Hannah too."

"Let's go," Hannah urged. "Please, Grandpapa. Percy's right."

"No!" he protested. "I must open it."

I could see it was useless to argue further with him, so I decided to humor him by doing as he said as quickly as possible, and to hope for the best.

The closet was locked, but luckily I had my little tools in my jacket pocket. I quickly picked the lock and when we looked in, I am sure Mr. Finermann was as surprised as I was.

3

Not one safe but five, all in a row and each small — no more than a cubic foot.

"My God!" he exclaimed. "Five!"

"What is this?" I asked, looking from the safes to Mr. Finermann and then to the safes again."

"Five safes to protect the one that is real. The one that has the thing. They are meant to confuse any thief with a puzzle that will take forever to solve."

"You mean to open all of them?"

"Yes. We'll be caught again for sure by the time we do that."

"Then, let's go. Time to highass for home," Hannah said, again tugging at the old man's good arm.

"No," he still protested, but clearly not knowing what to do. Happily, the screaming thug with the ruined knees had passed out and made no more noise.

I decided to reason with him. "Look Mr. Finermann, even if we do find the right safe, the odds are very great that it will not be the first we open. "Probability says we have a .20 chance of getting it right the first time, .25 on the second, and .33 on the third. Not good odds, eh? And besides, as you know it will take us too long — far too long — to open even more than one safe. We'll surely be caught."

"Good heavens! It could take us all night to work our way through bad guesses, but we must try," he insisted, this time with a tone of determination. "Percival, you have time to open one safe. You choose which one and may God bless your choice."

I looked at the safes.

"Do it, Percy," said Hannah.

"Well, *you* won't be able to open anything with a broken arm, but you can help me. I heard him moan with the pain from his arm. Then it came to me. Without consulting Mr. Finermann, I began to sniff and lick the top hinge on each safe, taking time between each to wipe my tongue on my sleeve.

"What in the name of... ?" — he cut himself short. But I said nothing until I had licked the last hinge.

"He's gone bloomin' crazy," I heard Hannah whisper. "I've expected this for some time. Now the strain has sent him round the bloody bend. He'll be lickin' the damn floor next."

"It's that safe," I said, pointing at the one on the left end. "That one, I believe."

Mr. Finermann gave me a sidelong look as if to ask if I was quite in my right mind. Hannah too.

"It's the safe they open all the time and its hinges taste of rancid hog lard," I explained. "The others — the decoys—don't need to have their hinges lubricated because they don't use them. But that one does. At least, that's my best guess."

He smiled. "It is indeed the best guess we can make, Percival. You are a genius, my boy."

"No he's not, Grandpapa. He's a damn lunatic."

Although *he* was right, I expected to be a dead genius in another five minutes or so. Still, with Mr. Finermann breathing heavily and groaning over my shoulder to give his advice, I knelt on the floor and taking tools from his bag that we had used before, I began to work on the combination. At first I tried the combination by simply listening at the door, but it was subtle and gave no indication. Then I resorted to our listening tools and that allowed me to read the working of the locking mechanism very well. It took time — too much time I felt — to figure my way past all the poor choices I could make, but in ten minutes I believed I had deveined the proper combination.

"I believe I have it," I said looking up at Mr. Finermann's anguished face.

"Then try it," he groaned. "Try it and God help us!" He seemed to sway a little and I feared he would pass out from the pain.

At that moment, and I don't know why, I wondered why on earth God would care and why I was opening the safe in the first place. I was merely there to help Mr. Finermann and it occurred to me that I did not know anything other about why I was in my predicament. Still, I worked the combination that my efforts had suggested and the door opened. At that moment, Mr. Finermann stepped forward, clearly because he knew what he was expecting to find in the safe.

He reached in and took out an iron box, with a lock that was easy to pick. In it, to my surprise, there was a small machine of sorts, with gears and some wires and other internal mechanisms that I could not see.

"What is it?" I asked.

"Never mind that, Percival. We must leave here quickly, or risk being apprehended again. Those men have friends who'll not stop at killing all of us for what we have done."

I was relieved that he now agreed with me that it was way past time to run for the tall grass.

We moved carefully through the house, expecting to be attacked by those 'friends' Mr. Finermann had worried about. Still, we reached the front door and struggled beyond, into a still and silent night.

As we emerged I took Mr. Finermann's good arm and guided him across the lawn, still leaning on me and still groaning. Hannah as usual clutched at my other arm.

When we reached the hedgerow, halfway to the road, I stopped with jolt to see a tall dark shadow suddenly step in front of us. At first it seemed to me that the figure was dazed and shaking, but then I felt the ground shake, like I would imagine a small quake. It continued to shake and as it did so, the figure advanced on us and began to glow. The shaking continued.

Meanwhile, I thought that I must be hallucinating again and thought to myself this was a fine time to have such a thing. But then I felt Hannah tugging at my arm and when I turned to look at her, I could tell that she was looking at me with fright. "Percy! What is it? What's the matter?" Then I knew she could only see my fright and that I could not move.

I turned again to the shadowy figure and as it advanced on us and it came more fully into sight, I gasped to see that it was Lovecroft. Now, however, he was growing to half again his normal size and somehow he seemed to emit a strange green glow.

"Go back!" he ordered. "Go back, Master St.-John!"

It was Lovecroft's voice for sure, but now it was somehow even fiercer and more hateful. Now, as he neared, I could also smell his stink, which was the same I had retched to smell in the basement of the tobacco shop.

As Hannah tugged even more forcefully at my arm, the specter began to glow even brighter, with the subtle green light and his eyes were white. Suddenly, he produced a long lizard-like tongue that he wagged from side-to-side.

Lovecroft — or, I should say the demon that Lovecroft truly was — raised his long, muscular arms and roared his anger at me — threatening to incinerate all of us with his hot breath, which now emitted a stink that was close to overpowering.

"Back!" he growled again. "Go back, Master St.-John, or I will turn you and the others to ash!"

As my fright and quandary about what to do peaked, I suddenly sensed — I guess that's the word — that a light had somehow appeared behind me. I turned and could see that it was indeed a blue light, like a blue fog, and out from that mist there emerged five figures, no taller than me. As they came toward me, I saw first that the figure in the center was Arthur, and as the others came into view, I did not recognize any of them.

I glanced immediately round to Lovecroft, who somehow seemed frozen in place by the new figures. As I looked back at Arthur and the others, they passed through and past Hannah and me like a wind. In an instant they were in front of us, facing Lovecroft.

Standing tall and fierce before him, Lovecroft's awful face turned to fright in an instant. Now, at the sight of Arthur and the others the creature that Lovecroft had become slowly melted with his horror, until he was reduced to a smoldering puddle of stinking, green slim on the ground in front of us.

A long moment passed, as we all looked at the puddle. Then, Arthur and the others turned to face us. I don't know how, but now I knew that the boys with Arthur were "the others" who Lovecroft had allow to die and who were buried "out back." Just as that thought came into my mind, I saw Arthur, looking into my eyes, smiled at me in that shy way he often smiled, and then he and the other faded into the blue fog and were soon gone.

Hannah said nothing, but tugged again at my arm, and of course this time I did not hesitate. Taking Mr. Finermann again by his good arm and with Hannah still grasping at my left arm, I guided the two of them toward the road.

Mr. Finermann moved slowly, moaning all the while, and I took my time to ensure that he did not fall and cripple himself even more. Soon we were through the hedge, in the street, with me carrying the tool bag with the little mechanism in it and supporting the old man. Once there, Mr. Finermann did not seem to know which way to go, but just then a coach turned up the street from the direction in which we were running, and immediately I knew we'd been caught. The trouble was that there were walls on either side of us and so the only thing to do was to retrace our steps.

"This way!" I shouted to Mr. Finermann, as I turned to run.

"Percival, NO!" I heard him shout after me. "Come back! Come back! Hannah, come back!"

I did not like to trust what I was hearing from him, but I could not abandon him. He was refusing what I thought best. I turned reluctantly and retraced my steps, and there we stood, waiting for the coach to stop and the villains, whoever they were, to point pistols in our faces again. I prepared to raise my hands and turn over our loot, such as it was.

Imagine my surprise when out from the coach stepped the big man, accompanied by what looked like the two gents who'd come with him to the shop. They ran toward us and as they reached him Mr. Finermann fell forward into the big man's arms. We all helped him toward the coach, Hannah and I flummoxed and not knowing what we were doing or what to expect next. All a mystery to me, but I was merely following where Mr. Finermann was going, or rather where he was being taken.

The coach driver hardly waited for the door to close before he whipped up down the street, in the general direction of Paddington Station, and then to points east. Meanwhile, Mr. Finermann, his eyes closed, moaned with each jolt of the coach and I thought almost passed out. Hannah's face was desperate, and with her you never knew when she might decide to bite someone.

"What's the matter?" the big man asked.

"Broke his arm," I answered, as the old man just groaned.

The big man quickly opened the roof trap and shouted to the coachee, "To St. Mary's and quick!"

The driver made a quick turn to the north and suddenly we were in the Edgware Road, heading back toward St. Mary's Hospital. Fortunately for Mr. Finermann the streets were empty at that hour and so our coach flew through Paddington. In all the while I sat quietly, observing and not being paid much attention by anyone. I held the tool bag on my lap, with the little machine inside, still not knowing much of what was happening, but now knowing that the gents seemed to care that Mr. Finermann was injured and that, I told myself, was a good thing.

On the other side, however, the more I observed the three, the more they looked to be thugs, and so I retained a modest suspicion that Mr. Finermann had somehow fallen in with criminals, who only wanted to keep him alive for some despicable reason. Then I began to worry that the fellow whose knees I had ruined might be a policeman who had apprehended Mr. Finermann. I swallowed hard.

The coach moved into the precincts of St. Mary's Hospital and fetched-up at a small building adjacent, which I took to be the infirmary the big man had named. When we arrived and descended from the coach, the three hauled Mr. Finermann out and carried him to a waiting gurney at the door. Hannah and I followed.

A Metropolitan Policeman standing out front seemed wary of the three, and so I braced for big trouble. Then, however, the big man took a wallet from his inside coat pocket and presented it, and the policeman stepped to attention. Odd that he would do that for a thug, so I began to have some confidence the three thugs were policemen too, or something closely resembling the coppers.

Inside, two sisters took Mr. Finermann in charge, and then a doctor and the three whatevers followed into an inner room. I spotted a bench in the lobby and that's where Hannah and I decided to camp, holding hands and waiting for results. I knew the docs could fix a broken arm, so that didn't worry me nearly as much as Mr. Finermann's age. I fretted that his heart might give out, especially when you considered all he'd been through that night. Even missing a night's sleep could take a toll on a man of his age and frailty.

As Hannah sobbed and clutched my hand, I sat silently, ruminating on such fears for what seemed forever, though I knew from the clock on the lobby wall that it had been only the best part of an hour. Meanwhile, Hannah's sobbing soon gave way to speech.

"Percy?"

"Yes."

"I want to tell you something."

"Yes."

"Well, I guess I should."

"Should what?"

"Should say it."

The continuing nature of our conversation was beginning to irritate, but I decided to give it one more chance.

"What do you wish to say, Hannah?"

"I'm sorry for the way I've treated you, Percy. I should have given you more the benefit of the doubt, like Grandpapa did. I stuck too long on my opinion that you are a criminal lunatic."

I hardly knew what to say to such an unexpected reversal of her opinions. In normal circumstances I might have told her to take a headlong run at the nearest wall, but thinking how her Grandpapa's situation must have pained her, I decided to be civil.

"Thank you, Hannah. It means a lot to me that you have changed your opinion of me," I said, squeezing her hand and smiling at her.

"Percy," she continued, clearly not finished.

"What were you waiting for back there at the house? It was if you were frozen by fear. It made me even more afraid."

Her question took me back. I knew in an instant that she and Mr. Finermann must not have seen the bloodcurdling spectacle that I had witnessed. While I puzzled what to say, she decided to explain it for me.

She gasped. "Percy, you must have been having a vision, probably occasioned by your weakened mind."

"Yes, that is almost certainly what happened. But unfortunately I don't remember myself."

She now gave me one of those Hannah looks, like she'd reconsidered he attitude toward me and was back to thinking I was indeed an incurable loon.

I turned away looking at my hands and we sat for a long moment in silence. I finally decided to say no more and let Hannah think that I had had a momentary lapse of sanity, probably because of fear. After all, it had been my hallucination.

Soon, the three coppers returned to the lobby, followed by the bobby. The big man looked at me, for the first time with a slight smile. At least, it was what I imagined a slight smile would look like on a face like his. Hard to tell actually.

"Tobias will be alright," he assured us. "He particularly wanted me to tell you that, young lady, because he knew you'd be worried about him. His arm is badly broken and his hand too, but he'll recover the use of both, says the doctor."

It was then I decided to ask what I'd been wondering about for a while.

"Please," I started, assuming my most innocent look, "Who are you and what have you and Mr. Finermann been doing with those men who broke his arm?"

The big man frowned and then sat on the bench beside Hannah, while the other two took the copper aside, well out of hearing.

"I suppose you should know something about what's happened. After all, you've been right in the thick of it and Tobias tells me he'd not have escaped without you, Percival. Your quick action."

I said nothing but drew a deep breath.

"We — the two others and I — are agents of Special Branch of Scotland Yard. Do you know what that is?"

"Yes. You're spies, eh? Or at least, that's what the newspapers say."

He took the credential from his inside pocket again and this time showed it to us. It said 'Special Branch' for sure, so I decided to believe him."

"Golly," said Hannah.

"Tobias is a secret operative of Special Branch," he continued. I gasped. "He does special work for us when there's a safe or vault needs opening. He's an expert, as you well know."

"Yes."

"Tonight he took on a particularly important job, and as you saw, he was caught. We thought the house would be empty, but that turned out to be a lot of bunk. That's when you interrupted and I might say that you saved his life. Those two blighters who'd caught him would surely have beaten him until he confessed and then killed him. They are that sort, eh?"

I swallowed hard. "Yes?" I knew Hannah, who stared wide-eyed as the big man continued, must have been buzzing with delight that her Grandpapa was a secret operative.

"Tobias had gone in tonight to retrieve a very important object, which we figured would be in a safe. We had good information, from one of the housemaids; where the room with the safe would be and we also figured there'd be no one home. That part of her information turned out to be Gawdawful, but then that happens in this business."

"What business?" I asked.

"The business of gaining secrets from foreign operatives. The house you entered last evening belongs to the Austrian Government. It's the home of an important diplomat at their Embassy in London. What's called a military *chargé d'affaires*."

I didn't know what that was, but I figured it was darn important, so I gave him a very knowing, "Oh, I see."

"Tobias passed out before he could tell us much about what happened, but we are pleased that you were able to help him out of there. I only wish he'd succeeded in his work because he has certainly suffered for it," the big man said, looking down and shaking his head.

I bucked up that I was finally able to tell him something he didn't know.

"But he did succeed."

"What!" he perked up.

I opened the tool sack beside me on the bench and took out the little machine. Holding it up to his face, his bushy eyebrows shot up about six inches, his eyes bulged and his mouth fell open, like a halibut preparing to eat a minnow. I'd swear his big red nose flashed a little brighter.

"What the... !" he exclaimed, taking the thing from my hand and continuing to stare at it, his mouth agape.

"I opened the safe and took it out. Mr. Finermann said that's what he wanted."

"You opened the safe?"

"Yes," I said, with that special look that said I was offended to be questioned about it.

"Percy's a bloody cracksman and a damn good one too. Grandpapa says he's a genius," Hannah insisted. I was pleased she didn't go on to say that I was also a little loony.

"I don't quite know what to say," the big man continued, now smiling. "But we will certainly say more later. For now, I have told the policeman out front to see to it that you are escorted back to Tobias' shop for the night and you'll hear more from us tomorrow, eh?"

"Alright," I said, thinking that we weren't going to have another choice.

CHAPTER TWENTY
WHEREIN I MEET THE SPECIAL BRANCH

1

I returned to the shop with the policeman, while Hannah had begged to remain at the hospital with her Grandpapa. The odd thing was that I realized that I still had not learned the name of the big man and his two cronies. I made a mental note to be sure to ask later. In the meantime, I continued to worry about Mr. Finermann. He was old — too darn old to be out at all hours doing what he was doing — and I wondered about his heart. I made another mental note to tell him that he ought to stay in the shop and stick to his business, instead of having midnight adventures breaking into safes. By the time I took to my cot that night my mental bulletin board had notes pasted all over it because there was much about the situation I did not know and needed to ask about.

But all of that was beside the point of something that troubled me even more, especially now that I worried less about Mr. Finermann. Cosmo was nowhere to be found. I told myself there must be some explanation for that and that he would turn up, proving that I was merely having another of my terrible imaginings.

Meanwhile, Hannah returned a few hours later. She didn't want to sleep upstairs without her Grandpapa. I let her sleep on the floor in my closet. I found it difficult once again to drift off to sleep. First, I wondered that neither Hannah nor her Grandpapa remembered seeing what I had clearly witnessed that night — how Lovecroft dissolved into the demon that he really was and then how Arthur and the others had dissolved him into a puddle of slime. But as soon as the thought of Arthur came into my mind, I immediately felt the same sensation of delight I had had when his blue figure had turned and smiled at me. There was only one meaning I could put on that smile. He was telling me that everything was now all right and that I needn't fret any longer that I had failed him. It was with this wonderful thought in my mind that I finally fell into a dreamless sleep.

Early next morning Hannah and I discussed what we should do. We decided that after a bit of breakfast we'd leg it to the hospital infirmary and try to see Mr. Finermann. First, however, it was clear Hannah had something on her mind. She was quieter than usual and frowned her way through breakfast. Before she could tell more of what was on her mind, however, the big man and his two cronies arrived, this time in a nice coach that stayed out front of the shop. As soon as he entered he introduced himself.

"I suppose I should tell you, Percival; my name's Fish. Jericho Fish. My two associates are DCIs Longman and Frederickson. We are all three agents of Scotland Yard's Special Branch. We've just spoken further with Tobias, as he recovers in St. Mary's. He told me the whole story — how you saved both him and his mission last evening. That was a fine piece of work — your handling the thugs who'd taken Tobias and then opening the proper safe. Fry me for an oyster if that isn't the first time I ever heard of someone using five safes to confuse a thief. Not a bad idea, but according to Tobias, it didn't stop you for long. That's the important thing."

"So, you've seen Mr. Finermann? How is he?"

"Progressing nicely, according to the sisters."

I exhaled a sigh of relief. Hannah let out a scream that I'm sure was heard in East London.

"As you say," I replied. "I managed to open the right safe. But what was that little machine Mr. Finermann wanted so badly? Didn't look like much to me."

Fish looked at the other two, as if to confer, but then answered himself, though a little reluctantly. They gave Hannah a glance too, considering whether they could speak in front of her. She just raised her chin and gave them one of those special Hannah looks — tilted her head to one side and frowned.

"It was a mechanism of foreign origin that is thought to be a very important part of a new kind of undersea vessel that one of our foreign adversaries is developing. Our government very particularly wanted to get a good look at it and maybe to duplicate it. Now, thanks to you, we'll be able to do just that. Thanks to you and Tobias, I should say.

"Hannah too," I reminded him.

"Aye. Hannah too," he agreed, smiling.

"I'm darn pleased to know that Mr. Finermann is on the mend and will be home soon," I said, "but I'll wager it's going to take a while for his arm and hand to be good as new, eh?"

"I'll warrant that is so," Fish nodded and then paused as if to consider what he wanted to say next. He turned to me.

"Err... there *is* one thing... eh... Particularly... that we've come to see you about, Percival — one thing beyond telling you about Tobias and his recovery, that is. We have been... eh... our superiors have suggested that we might bring you to Special Branch because... well, they wish to question you about some things and possibly to discuss some things with you. That's why we've come so early."

I hadn't expected such a question and it gave me pause. My guilty imagination went racing through all sorts of things the police might want to question me about. But on quick reflection, I couldn't think of anything I'd done that might prompt that sort of thing, except perhaps that I'd stolen all Reverend Lovecroft's loot. I decided I was probably going to be arrested for that one, finally, but there wasn't much use to run now.

"Alright, I'll come," I said with a tone of sullen resignation. "I don't suppose I have much choice. But, will you see that Hannah gets to the hospital to see her Grandpapa?"

"Of course. Tobias particularly wants to see her. He also wants to keep the shop open and says he'll trust you to do that, while he recovers."

Fish at first looked a little puzzled, but quickly moved toward the door. I took off my shop apron and followed.

2

As we glided through the early morning congestion of wagons, coaches, and carriages, not to mention the occasional bicyclist and motor, I looked out and wondered where we were going. Wherever it turned out to be, I assured myself, it would probably be a surprise. Then I was sure because we headed east into central London and soon entered the precincts of Whitehall and the great complex of imposing government buildings where the headquarters of the Metropolitan Police was located.

Now, however, we proceeded without stopping, into East London. To my surprise we fetched-up at the tobacco shop where the big man — Fish — had disappeared when I'd followed him. I shuddered to think of going in — remembering the five green demons. The coach driver waited as we entered the shop, were a little man with lots of black hair and a round head with a pink face pasted on it stood smiling behind a counter lined with tobacco jars. Fish nodded to him as we entered and then proceeded through a curtain to the back of the shop and to the familiar door that led downstairs to the basement. Once there, while I glanced warily at the wall with the bench — half expecting to see what I had seen before — Fish pulled aside the cupboard, which moved easily to reveal a passage.

"What's this?" I finally asked, thinking I was being taken somewhere that would do me no good.

"This is an access to the building across the street — the one that says London Water and Sewers Authority. It's really Special Branch headquarters. The tunnel is used by a special group of people, who do not want their association with us to be known and who the SB wants to keep unknown too. You might call them clandestine employees of the Special Branch.

"Oh," I said, pretending to understand fully what he meant.

We walked through the dimly lighted passage for more than a hundred yards; in what direction I could not tell. Finally, we came to an ordinary-looking door, which Fish unlocked and which opened into a well-lighted but empty room. The little room's door, however, gave access to a very nice, broad corridor lined with doors, where people walked to and fro. The big man led me along the passage to a stairs, which took us up three floors to a top suite of offices. We came to a door.

"Go in there and wash your hands and brush aside your hair, lad. You're about to meet someone important and you'll want to look your best."

I did as he told, and found a small lavatory, with a washbasin and mirror. It took only a minute or two the spruce-up, and then I followed him to a nearby door. It said merely "Director."

When we entered there sat a thin, severe-looking young woman with a long face and bulging eyes. She gave me a slightly discordant look up and down and then made a face as if she'd just swallowed a fly.

"Master St.-John to see Sir Joshua," said Fish.

The woman rose and entered an office with large, double doors. She emerged in less than a minute and holding open one door, and as we entered closed it behind us. And there we stood, in front of a small man at a large desk. "Sir, this is Master Percival St.-John. Percival, meet Sir Joshua Reagan, Director of Special Branch."

The little man, whose head was entirely bald and narrow, wore a monocle in his right eye. He smiled broadly to see me. "Come in! Come in!" he beamed, rising and inviting both Fish and me to sit in large chairs near his desk.

"Master St.-John, I have just finished reading the report of your actions concerning the mission that Tobias Finermann had undertaken for Special Branch last night. It was a fine piece of work if I do say, and we are of course grateful for your actions. You may not know the half of it, lad, but you not only saved a good man's life — you also salvaged a very important effort that has brought great merit to Special Branch and of course a significant gain to His Majesty's Government."

All this sat pretty well with me. It sounded like I was not going to be arrested for stealing all Reverend Lovecroft's loot, and I could now hope Sir Joshua was leading up to putting a few quid in my pocket for my service, if it had been all that useful. I was thinking that I could use a bit of the ready just then because the stash under my cot was getting thin of late, partly because we had bought the bicycle. Just then, however, he paused, as if to consider carefully what he intended to say next. I sensed that my chances of coming into some new money were slipping away.

"I've also just talked on the telephone with the Home Secretary, Master St.-John, because it is he who must decide upon such things." I noticed that Sir Joshua had an odd way of moving his nose from side to side before he spoke.

"Oh?" I asked. "What things?" And I wasn't exactly sure who this Home Secretary blighter was, but he sounded an important cove.

"Well, the long and short of it is that Fish here has proposed that your work was such that Special Branch should make use of your talents in the future. This is particularly so in as much as Mr. Finermann has told us that he feels he's insufficiently spry to undertake such work in the future."

"Make use of my talents?"

"Yes. Fish believes that you can certainly take Finermann's place in our scheme of things. You know, undertaking the sort of jobs that Finermann has done for us.

And, I might add that Tobias has agreed. Says you are a corker of a safeman, in fact. He adds that you have plenty of experience as a... well... err... as a thief."

"You mean breaking into safes in the middle of the night and looting what's in them," I said, making sure we both had the same thing in mind. Fish shifted uneasily in his chair from one cheek to the other.

Sir Joshua sniffed a bit and then stiffened, wriggling his nose so violently that the monocle jumped from his eye. "Exactly. To take Finermann's place in those sorts of activities," he said, restoring the monocle.

"And Mr. Finermann says he's alright with this?" I asked.

"Indeed. Says you may continue to work in his shop and he'll even make allowance for you to do our little jobs, from time to time. As he has done."

"How much?" I asked, abruptly.

Sir Joshua harrumphed a bit and then sniffed again. His nose wriggled.

"Do you mean to ask how much you'll be paid for your services?"

"Yes, that's exactly what I mean. How much is the work worth to you?"

"To begin, £600 per year, with more to come depending on circumstances."

"Blimey!" I said, my mouth gaping.

"Aye, lad. It's a generous sum, but it's for some important work," Fish explained. "And dangerous too, as you've seen. You'll earn every penny of it, I'll warrant. And you already know from what you saw the other night that there's no denyin' the danger."

Sir Joshua leaned back in his chair, looking at his hands thoughtfully. He remained silent for a while, as Fish and I exchanged puzzled glances.

"There *is* one difficulty," he finally said, looking up and frowning. "Not that I think it will matter in the long run, but it troubles the Home Secretary, so ———."

Aye, I thought to myself, *this is where they give me a drubbing about the awful things I did to Reverend Lovecroft.* Sir Joshua fell into another silence.

"It's your grandfather," he finally said, with a sigh.

I'm sure my mouth fell open again.

"My grandfather? My grandfather refuses to have anything to do with me," I said, surprised that he had even come up in our talk. "He hated my mother and even rejected my father because he'd married her. And I don't much wish to associate with him, either," I explained.

"Yes, we know all that. You see, the Home Secretary has been in contact with him, because of the... well, because of the work Special Branch has for you. Don't you see?"

"But what does my grandfather have to do with anything?" I wondered aloud.

"It's not that he wishes to involve himself. He clearly does not. But, it is because of who he is and who you are, don't you see."

I was puzzled and gave a look that showed it. Fish frowned.

"As you doubtless know, your grandfather is the Earl of Tattershall. He sits in the bloomin' House of Lords. And no matter his attitude toward you, Percival. You are his only heir and one day you will inherit the title and the seat. Surely you know that."

I did in fact. My father had told me as much because *he* expected to inherit. But I couldn't see how it made any difference, so I asked. "How does that make any difference? What does the Home Secretary care about my grandfather?"

"It merely gives him pause and a certain amount of anxiety, because... eh... well, you see, because things could go badly for you. You could be captured or even killed in doing what we have in mind and that could cause a bit of a sticky wicket... for His Majesty's Government, don't you see."

"Yes. I see," I agreed, noting that the Home Secretary's concern was *not* for me being killed or captured. Still, there was that £600 per year to be considered and that was what I had my eye on. That, and all the excitement to be had doing what Mr. Finermann had been doing. By this time, I enjoyed opening safes like nothing else and the challenge of opening the toughest of them was inviting.

"So where do things stand, sir?" Fish asked. I was wondering that myself.

Sir Joshua hesitated, while his nose jumped about. "I don't quite know. There'll need to be some further conversation between the Home Secretary and others before a decision can be made. It will take a while, I'm sure. Meanwhile," he turned to me, "go back to your shop, young Percival. Take care you don't get in any trouble, and by that, I mean no opening safes on your own account. And, take good care of Finermann. He will be home in a few days and will need rest and care."

I nodded to all he'd said, and that was the signal for Fish to lead me out, past the young, frowning woman, and through the passages to the tobacco shop.

3

I heard nothing from Fish and Special Branch for the next weeks. Mr. Finermann returned in three days and as I expected, took to his bed. Special Branch assigned a nurse — a big, happy woman of about fifty years named Mrs. Proctor — to look after his needs and particularly to cook for him. Mrs. Wambly took a hand also, of course.

I kept up the shop, and all the while missed Cosmo who had also not returned. In another week the old man was on his feet, though with a bandage on his arm and hand. Still, he was able to work at his bench and to oversee what I was doing and to greet customers who continued to come at about the same pace. Business was good.

Just as I doubted I'd ever see him again, Fish came to the shop, wearing a stern face.

"Sir Joshua wishes to see you, Percival. Clean yourself up and come along, lad," he ordered. I did as he told, and within the hour we were through the tobacco shop and in Sir Joshua's bureau. The Director of SB seemed pleased to see us.

"Come in. Do come in," he invited, showing us the chairs we'd occupied previously, while he continued to sit at his desk wriggling his nose happily.

"Well, Master St.-John, I have some news to impart. Good news, I think. The Home Secretary has conferred with others — the Prime Minister among them, I assume — and he has now approved your work for Special Branch. He has assessed the risks and accepts them, eh."

It was now that I decided to give voice to something that I'd been considering for several days.

"I'll do your work, Sir Joshua, but on one further condition."

"Oh?" he said, coming forward in his chair, his eyes narrow.

"Yes. I will do the work you wish if Special Branch and the Government will permit me one thing."

Sir Joshua looked at Fish, who then looked at me.

"What is that?" he asked, guardedly, again glancing at Fish and wriggling his nose.

"I want Scotland Yard to open a special investigation into my father's murder. I want you to find the foul blisters who killed him and bring them to the gallows."

Sir Joshua and Fish exchanged more questioning glances and then Sir Joshua spoke.

"Agreed! We will open that investigation as soon as possible and keep it open as long as it takes to find the villains. How's that, Master Percival?"

All of that seemed to me the best possible outcome. I would continue working side-by-side with Mr. Finermann in his shop and we could continue our friendship just as in the past. My father's killers would be brought to the scaffold. And, I was also relieved that nothing had been said about robbing Reverend Lovecroft of his loot.

Still smiling as he rose from his desk, Sir Joshua told me to return to the shop and resume my work, helping Mr. Finermann as much as possible. "You will hear from SB in due course."

Fish escorted me through the passages and then into the tobacco shop. Once on the street, where the coach waited, he stopped as if he'd forgotten something.

"When you are summoned to Special Branch, Percival, you'll come here as usual and present your credential to the tobacconist — then proceed through the passages, just as we have done."

"My credential?" I asked.

"Oh yes. I have it here, somewhere," he explained, searching his coat pockets. "Ah yes. Here you have it," he said handing it to me. I took it without looking and boarded the coach that would take me to the lock shop. I worried about keeping it open while Mr. Finermann recovered his health.

As I closed the coach door I gasped and then almost shouted out loud. Cosmo sat on the facing seat. I smiled and he seemed to smile back at me.

He said nothing as our coach rolled through central London, toward the Edgware Road, so I decided to examine the credential Fish had given me.

I almost laughed out loud to read it. "Aye lad. That's you," said Cosmo, smiling his wicked grin.

Beneath the seal and words Special Branch, it said:

Percival Saint-John
Codename: Midnight Boy

HISTRIA BOOKS

Other outstanding books for young adult readers:

For these and many other great books visit

HistriaBooks.com